# THE BOXCAR CHILDREN®

### CREATED BY
### GERTRUDE CHANDLER WARNER

# CREEPY CLUES SPECIAL

FEATURING

## THE MYSTERY OF THE STOLEN SWORD
1–115

## THE VAMPIRE MYSTERY
117–216

## HIDDEN IN THE HAUNTED SCHOOL

ALBERT WHITMAN & COMPANY
CHICAGO, ILLINOIS

The Boxcar Children Creepy Clues Special
created by Gertrude Chandler Warner.

Copyright © 2017 by Albert Whitman & Company
Published in 2017 by Albert Whitman & Company

ISBN 978-0-8075-2848-8

Printed in the United States of America
10 9 8 7 6 5 4 3 2 1 LB 22 21 20 19 18 17

Cover art by Anthony VanArsdale
Interior illustrations by Charles Tang, Robert Papp, and Anthony VanArsdale

Visit the Boxcar Children online at www.boxcarchildren.com.
For more information about Albert Whitman & Company,
visit our website at www.albertwhitman.com.

# THE BOXCAR CHILDREN

BOOK 67

BY
GERTRUDE
CHANDLER
WARNER

# THE MYSTERY OF THE STOLEN SWORD

ILLUSTRATED BY
CHARLES TANG

# Contents

**CHAPTER 1**

# A Ghost Story

Six-year-old Benny Alden stood outside his house in Greenfield, watching the moonrise. An owl hooted. Oak and maple trees rustled in the wind, and a few raindrops sprinkled Benny on the nose.

Benny shivered. In the moonlight, his front yard looked so spooky, he was almost sure he could see a ghost. And Benny definitely believed in ghosts.

It was early November, just a few days after Halloween. The leaves on the trees were yellow and brown, and many of the branches were almost bare. In the mornings, frost lay on the ground. The perfect season for ghosts, Benny thought.

"Benny, dinner's ready!" called a familiar voice. It was Benny's ten-year-old sister, Violet.

"Coming!" Benny called back. He took one more look at the moon before he raced inside.

"I'm starving," Benny announced to his family, who were already beginning to seat themselves at the long dining room table.

"You're always hungry, Benny," Henry reminded him with a smile. Henry was Benny's fourteen-year-old brother, and he could never resist teasing Benny a little.

Tonight Mrs. McGregor, the Aldens' housekeeper, had made one of Benny's favorite meals: spaghetti and meatballs, and her special homemade brownies for dessert.

Benny quickly slid into his seat next to his sister Jessie.

"How many meatballs, Benny?" asked Jessie as she put spaghetti on Benny's plate.

"Oh, maybe four," Benny answered.

"We can always count on you to have a good appetite, Benny," Grandfather remarked.

"I'll say," Henry agreed.

Jessie laughed but gave Benny all the meatballs he wanted. At age twelve, Jessie was the oldest girl

in her family, and she often acted like a mother to her orphaned brothers and sister.

After their parents died, Henry, Jessie, Violet, and Benny had lived in an abandoned boxcar in the woods because they thought they had nowhere else to go. They did not know that their grandfather was looking everywhere for them. When he finally found his missing grandchildren, he was overjoyed. And he lost no time inviting them to live with him—an offer the Aldens were happy to accept. Henry, Jessie, Violet, and Benny were especially pleased that Grandfather let them bring the old boxcar to his house too. It was now in Grandfather's backyard, and the children often used it as a playhouse on rainy days.

Outside, the wind shook the trees, and a branch banged against the house.

Violet shuddered. "It's awfully windy tonight. Is there a storm coming?"

As if in answer, the lights in the house flickered but did not go out.

"The papers did say there would be a storm," Grandfather told his family as he stirred his tea.

"The kind with lots of thunder and lightning?" Benny asked hopefully.

"Nothing that dramatic, I'm afraid," Grandfather said.

"That's good." Violet sounded relieved. She looked around the dining room. The chandelier cast a soft glow on the walls and over the red-and-white-checked tablecloth. The smell of homemade tomato sauce mingled with that of the brownies baking in the oven.

As Mrs. McGregor cleared away the dinner plates, Grandfather leaned back in his chair. "I have some news," he told his grandchildren.

"What?" asked Benny, holding his cup in midair.

"Well..." Grandfather began slowly. "My friend Seymour Curtis called today. He'd like us to come visit him on his farm sometime this month."

"Is he the one who's always sending us fruit from his orchard?" asked Henry.

"He's the one," Grandfather answered, nodding.

"In fact," Mrs. McGregor added, "we just received a crate of apples from him this afternoon. I'll probably make apple pies with some of them tomorrow."

"Mmm," said Violet and Benny, almost in unison.

"Are there animals on this farm?" Benny wanted to know. "Or do they just grow fruit up there?"

"Oh, there are animals, Benny," his grandfather assured him. "The main business is the orchard, of course, but Seymour also keeps a few horses, cows, and a goat."

Benny beamed.

"And you know what else is on the farm?" Grandfather asked, looking at Benny.

"What?" Henry asked, just as eager to know.

"Well," Grandfather continued, "the orchard is supposedly haunted. At least that's what the townspeople think!"

Benny's eyes widened. "You mean there's a ghost?"

"Sort of," Grandfather said. "Everyone thinks the ghost of one of Seymour's ancestors haunts the farm—an ancestor who mysteriously vanished in the apple orchard one day and was never seen again."

"Oh, that's creepy!" Jessie exclaimed. "How long ago did this happen?"

# A Ghost Story

"Oh, in the 1850s," answered Grandfather as the lights flickered overhead and the wind whipped the rain against the windowpanes. "In fact, he disappeared on a windy, rainy day like this. It was on the day after Halloween, I believe."

"And no one knows what happened to him?" Jessie couldn't believe it.

Grandfather shook his head. "No, no one ever found out."

"Who was this ancestor?" Henry wanted to know. "And why did he just disappear like that? Was he running away from something? Or was it some kind of Halloween joke?"

"It wasn't much of a joke if no one ever saw him again," Violet remarked.

Grandfather leaned back in his chair. "Well, it's a long story," he began. "It all started in the middle of the last century when the farmhouse was first built."

Benny sat up straighter. He did not want to miss a word.

"The man who built the farm was an ancestor named Gideon Curtis, and he was rather eccentric."

"Ec-what?" asked Benny.

"Eccentric," Grandfather repeated. "He did some unusual things. For instance, he collected suits of armor and old swords, which he kept in a secret passageway he built in his farmhouse."

"Wow," said Benny. He was so interested in his grandfather's story, he was not even eating the brownie in front of him.

"This collection was very valuable," Grandfather continued. "So valuable that other people in Gideon's family wanted a share of it. One day, a relative from Virginia, a man named Joshua Curtis, came to visit Gideon. Joshua insisted that Gideon give him some swords from his collection, swords Joshua said belonged to his side of the family."

"Did they?" Jessie wondered aloud.

Grandfather shook his head. "Gideon didn't think so. He told Joshua he had no rightful claim to the swords. Joshua became very angry. He threatened Gideon and his family. Then he stormed out of the house, without any of his things, not even his coat. He walked into the orchard, and no one ever saw him again. It was as if he vanished."

"But people went out looking for him, didn't they?" Henry asked. He had barely touched his brownie, either.

"Oh, yes," Grandfather said as he poured cream into his tea. "Gideon and several men formed a search party. They looked for hours and hours. But no one ever found a trace of the man."

"Didn't he leave footprints?" Benny wanted to know.

"I'm sure he did," said Grandfather. "But none that ever led to his whereabouts. The townspeople believe that Joshua's ghost still haunts the orchard. And whenever Seymour has a poor harvest or other trouble on the farm, people blame the ghost. They say it's Joshua's revenge."

Benny's eyes grew very round. "You know, ghosts don't leave footprints," he informed his family. "Maybe that's why no one could find any sign of Joshua in the orchard."

"At that point he wasn't a ghost yet, Benny!" Jessie said, laughing.

"Did the ghost—I mean did Joshua—have a family in Virginia?" Violet asked.

"No, he never married and never had any children," Grandfather answered.

"How was Joshua related to Gideon?" Henry wondered as he poured more tea into his mug.

"They were cousins."

"How strange that Joshua just disappeared like that," Violet said. "I wonder what could have happened to him."

"It is an odd story," Grandfather agreed.

"Has anyone seen this ghost?" Henry wanted to know. "I mean, what makes people think the farm is haunted?"

Grandfather swallowed before he answered. "Some of the farmhands have heard strange noises in the orchard—leaves rustling even when there's no wind, the sound of twigs breaking in the underbrush, noises like that. Of course, it could just be some animal that people are hearing," Grandfather said.

Everyone nodded, except Benny. "I bet it's really a ghost," he insisted.

"We'll see," Grandfather said, chuckling.

"So when are we visiting?" Jessie wanted to know.

## A Ghost Story

"We'll leave the day after tomorrow," Grandfather answered.

"Mmm," said Benny, taking a bite of his brownie.

# CHAPTER 2

# The Orchard

"Grandfather, we have to turn right at the next road," Jessie said. She sat in the front of the station wagon with a map unfolded in her lap.

The Aldens had been driving for almost three hours. It was now noon—"time for lunch," Benny reminded everyone. Watch, who was lying in the very back, thumped his tail.

"See, Watch is hungry too," Benny announced.

"We'll be at the orchard by lunchtime," Grandfather said as he turned onto a narrow winding road. Acres and acres of fruit trees seemed to stretch for miles, broken only by fields where horses and cows grazed.

"Wow, there are a lot of orchards around here,"

Jessie commented. "All apples?"

"All apples," Grandfather answered.

"There's nothing on the trees now." Benny sounded disappointed as he looked at all the bare fruit trees.

"All the apples have been picked by this time," Grandfather explained. "Now Seymour is probably busy pruning the trees and cleaning up things around the barn."

"Does he need our help?" Benny asked.

"I'm sure Seymour would appreciate any help," Grandfather answered. "But this isn't a working vacation."

"Except that we have to look for the ghost," Benny reminded his family.

"And we can help feed the animals," Jessie suggested.

"Yes, you can probably do that," said Grandfather as he turned onto a dirt road. "You can see the Curtis farm up ahead," he informed his grandchildren as he pointed to a big red barn in the distance. Around the barn was a big house and a long, low shed.

"It looks like all the buildings on the farm are

connected," Henry observed. Grandfather was driving slowly now because there were deep ruts in the narrow dirt road.

"They are," Grandfather answered as he steered the car around a jagged rock in the road. "Farms that were built more than a hundred years ago often had connected buildings. They made for easy passage in the wintertime during those blinding snowstorms."

"Where is the secret passageway?" Benny wanted to know.

"Ah, that I'll let you find for yourself," Grandfather answered, "but I'll give you a hint. The secret passageway is underground."

"Underground," Benny repeated. He looked as if he didn't really believe it.

"Oh, look, a pumpkin patch," exclaimed Violet, pointing, "and there're still pumpkins in it."

"They're huge," Jessie commented.

The Aldens were now passing a pasture where two horses pranced very close to the barn.

"And we're here," Grandfather announced as he pulled the station wagon up to the big house—a two-story white building with green shutters and a wide wraparound porch.

Benny was the first one out of the car, with Watch at his heels.

"Well, hello, old friend," a deep voice boomed behind them.

Grandfather turned around and rushed to greet an elderly man with silvery hair, rosy cheeks, and bright blue eyes. "I saw you drive up from the barn," the man said. "I don't move as fast as I used to, or I would have been up here to greet you before you got out of the car."

Grandfather laughed and shook his head. "You certainly haven't changed, Seymour. It sure is good to see you."

"And these must be your grandchildren," Seymour said.

Grandfather nodded and proudly introduced Henry, Jessie, Violet, Benny, and Watch, who all shook the farmer's hand (including Watch!).

Though frail-looking, Mr. Curtis had a very firm handshake. "Please call me Seymour," the farmer insisted. "None of that Mr. Curtis nonsense. Your

grandfather and I have known each other since we were six years old."

"We met in first grade," Grandfather explained as he followed his friend up to the house.

The Aldens entered a small living room with a low ceiling and a worn wooden floor, covered with a small Oriental rug.

"This way," said Seymour, gesturing toward the big kitchen where his wife, Rose, was at the stove stirring a big pot of stew.

Already seated at the long wooden table in front of the stove were two middle-aged men.

"These are my farmhands," Seymour said as he introduced them to the Aldens. "Mike Johnson and Jeff Wilson have been working for me ever since they were in high school." They were both tall, big-boned men with dark curly hair and blue eyes. Henry noticed Mike had especially large feet, and he wore thick hiking boots. Jeff wore a pair of worn red sneakers. The two men looked a lot alike. The Aldens were not surprised to learn they were cousins.

"Will you be here long?" Jeff asked. Jeff had a wide smile and large white teeth.

"The Aldens are welcome to stay as long as they like," Seymour said. "Goodness knows, I've been trying to get my old friend up here for years now, but he's always been too busy."

Grandfather laughed. "We'll probably stay a week or two," he answered.

"Well, we'll have to put you to work," Jeff said, addressing Henry as he spoke. "We could show you around the farm, and you could help us bale some hay, if you feel like working."

"I could help too," said Benny.

"Nah, you'd just be in the way," Mike muttered. Benny just stared at the farmhand, too hurt and surprised to say anything more. The others didn't seem to have heard Mike's comment.

"Lunch is ready," Rose announced as she pulled a big tray of warm biscuits out of the oven.

"Oh, homemade buttermilk biscuits. My favorite," said Grandfather, rubbing his hands together. "Did I ever tell you that Rose makes the best biscuits in New England?" he asked his grandchildren.

"Now, James," Rose protested, laughing, "that's an exaggeration." But she looked pleased.

# The Orchard

"Everything smells wonderful," said Jessie.

"Food's always good here," Jeff agreed as he heaped stew on his plate. "It keeps Mike and me working here."

"We had a mighty good harvest this year," Mike was telling Grandfather. "Especially with the Baldwins."

"The Northern Spy did well too," Seymour added.

Benny perked up. "There's an apple called Northern Spy?"

"There sure is, son. You'll have to taste one before you leave," Seymour answered.

"Sure, I'll taste almost anything," Benny said.

"So the orchard is doing very well, Seymour," Grandfather remarked.

"Yes, the orchard is," Seymour said slowly, "but we've been having some other troubles." At this point he exchanged a look with his wife, who was frowning.

"I have to tell them, Rose," Seymour said. "James is one of my best friends."

"But they only just arrived," Rose protested.

"What is this all about?" asked Jeff. By now, everyone at the table was looking at Seymour, who was shaking his head sadly.

"Well, the truth is," Seymour began, choosing his words carefully, "we're being robbed."

"No!" Jeff exclaimed, while Mike whistled under his breath.

## CHAPTER 3

# The Missing Letters

"You mean someone is stealing your fruit?" Benny asked.

Seymour actually smiled. "No, nothing like that." He cleared his throat. "The fact is, someone is stealing our antiques—not the furniture, but smaller things like my stamp collection and some old family letters."

"Oh, no, Seymour," Grandfather said. "Your stamp collection was very valuable."

Seymour put down his fork. "It was," he agreed. "And so were some of those letters—at least to me. A lot of them dated from the Civil War."

"Were there any letters from the ghost?" asked Benny.

Seymour looked puzzled, but only for a moment. "Oh, you mean Joshua," he said, chuckling a little. "I see your grandfather has told you all the family history."

"Everyone for miles around knows about Joshua's ghost," Mike reminded the farmer.

"I suppose they do," Seymour agreed as he stirred his coffee. "But to answer your question, Benny, yes, some letters from Joshua were taken, along with Gideon's diary. Gideon was one of my ancestors, the one who built this farm," the farmer added, looking at the Aldens.

"Oh, we know about Gideon," Benny said.

Seymour looked at Grandfather and raised his eyebrows. "I can see you prepared your grandchildren well for this visit," he said.

"But we should be glad you didn't lose all of Gideon's letters," Rose reminded her husband as she handed him a piece of homemade apple pie for dessert.

"No, I have a few left. There are plenty of old letters in this house, some I haven't even read yet," Seymour remarked.

# The Missing Letters

"Seymour, why didn't you tell us about this? When did these robberies take place?" Jeff wanted to know.

Seymour looked at his farmhand. "I didn't notice the missing letters until last night," he said. "And as for the stamp collection, well, I think it disappeared maybe a week ago."

"You should have told us," Jeff persisted.

Seymour looked down at his hands. "Well, the truth is, I, uh, had to make sure those things really were missing. You know how forgetful I can be in my old age."

Jeff nodded, but he looked troubled. "Did you call the police?" he asked.

"I did. They came over to check things out."

"They told us there had been some other robberies nearby, in Chassell," Rose said. "Chassell is the nearest big town," she explained to the Aldens. "The thieves only took small items—old photographs, paintings, antique jewelry, things like that."

"So these thieves want antiques," Jeff said.

"Apparently so." Seymour sounded grim. "I just worry they'll take some of the old swords. But I think they're safe enough in the secret passageway."

"Are you sure?" Jeff asked, looking doubtful. "Everyone who's ever worked on the farm knows about the secret passageway. I wouldn't be surprised if most of the town knew about it too."

"That's true," said Seymour, frowning. "But only the farmworkers and some of my relatives know how to get inside it."

Benny perked up. "You mean the passageway has a secret entrance?"

Seymour nodded. "It has two secret entrances in fact."

"And all the people who work on the farm know how to get inside the passageway?" Henry asked.

"Yes, they would," Seymour answered.

"The only other people who know are my children and grandchildren, and they're sworn to secrecy. The entrance to the passageway has always been a farm secret."

"I guess you can't be too careful," said Jeff as he rose from his seat to stretch his arms. "I'm really sorry this happened, Seymour. Let me know if there's anything I can do to help."

"I will, Jeff, thank you."

"Well, Mike and I should be getting back to work. There's still a lot of clearing and pruning to do."

Mike looked at his hands. He had grown even more quiet during dessert and seemed very upset about the robberies. At last he sighed and rose, thanking the Curtises for lunch.

"Oh, you're welcome, Mike," Rose said.

Mike merely nodded and followed Jeff out the door.

Seymour watched them leave, stirring his coffee. He waited until the farmhands were out of sight before turning to the Aldens.

"You know, I have something to confess," Seymour began as Rose cleared the plates from the table with Violet and Benny's help. "This isn't easy for me to say, but the reason I didn't tell Jeff and Mike about these robberies right away is that, well, I just don't know what to think."

"What do you mean?" Grandfather asked.

Seymour sighed and looked close to tears. "Well, it's just that whoever did those robberies knows a lot about me and where I keep my things. I just can't help thinking that the burglar is someone I know pretty well."

"But, Seymour, surely you don't suspect Jeff and Mike. They've been working for you for years, ever since they were boys," Rose said.

"No, I don't believe it could be them, but I do employ other farmhands to help during the picking season."

"Who?" Jessie wanted to know.

"Well, this fall I had two high school students, Veronica and Martin. You'll meet them while you're here—they still help me out around the farm. They're good kids. I know their parents and grandparents."

"You know, Seymour, it's entirely possible this robbery is tied to the other antique robberies in town. It may not be anyone we know at all," Rose said.

"I wish I could believe that." Seymour sounded sad. "I hate to be in the position of suspecting everyone who works around here. But that stamp collection was in a secret drawer in my desk. And nothing else was touched. The thief knew just where to look."

"You've told your farmhands about your secret drawer?" Grandfather asked.

"Well, yes. I like to show that old desk to the people who come in. And Jeff and Mike have seen my stamp collection."

"Did the others know where your stamp collection was?" Jessie asked as she handed Benny more dishes to take off the table.

Seymour scratched his head. "Well, I told Veronica about it. She collects stamps too."

"I don't think we should jump to any conclusions until we have more evidence," Rose suggested. "You know that's what the police said."

"Right," said Seymour. "My wife is the down-to-earth one," he told the Aldens. "She always talks good sense." The farmer rose slowly. "Who would like to take a walk around the farm?" he asked.

"Me." Benny was the first to answer. "Can we see the secret passageway too?"

"Follow me," Seymour said, walking toward the door.

"Oh, Seymour, before you go, why don't you show the Aldens where their rooms are. They may want to unpack, or at least unload their belongings from the car. They've only just arrived."

"Good idea," said Seymour. "I told you Rose is the sensible one."

Everyone laughed.

The bedrooms were all upstairs on the second floor. Jessie and Violet had a fireplace and a four-poster bed in their room. Henry and Benny shared a corner room with built-in beds and bookcases.

"This is like a ship's cabin," Henry said happily when he saw it.

The Aldens unpacked quickly, and before long they were following Seymour outside toward the barn.

On the way, they passed a long vegetable garden guarded by a scarecrow made from sticks and straw. He wore a flannel shirt, loose denim pants, and a black felt hat.

"This is a great scarecrow," Benny remarked.

Seymour chuckled. "He sure comes in handy in the summer when he keeps the crows from eating all our vegetables."

## The Missing Letters

One side of the old red barn was filled with hay, and the other had stalls for two horses, three cows, and a goat named Elvira.

"You watch out for Elvira," the farmer warned the Aldens. "She'll eat anything in sight, even the shirt off your back, if you're not careful."

Benny giggled.

"I'm serious," Seymour said. "She's been known to nibble on laundry that's hanging outside to dry. And she eats everyone's food." Seymour shook his head and gave Elvira a playful pat.

"How often do you feed the animals?" Jessie wanted to know.

"Twice a day, now that winter's coming on," the farmer answered. "Early in the morning, and then again in the late afternoon. And sometimes they also get snacks during the day." Seymour reached into his pocket for two cubes of sugar, which he handed to Benny.

"Here, son, you can give these to the horses. They're outside," Seymour said, leading the way out to the pasture.

Once outside, Benny walked over to look at the

two horses who were grazing near the fence. "They don't bite, do they?" Benny wanted to know.

"Nah, they're tame as can be," the farmer assured him. The horses moved closer to Benny, and Benny promptly took a few steps backward, away from the fence.

"No need to be afraid," Seymour said. He reached through the fence to pat the white horse on the nose. "This one is called Hazel," he told the Aldens.

"Hazel?" Violet asked, a little puzzled.

"Her eyes are hazel," the farmer answered.

"And this one here"—Seymour pointed to her gray companion—"is Mister Mist."

Violet put her hand through the fence to stroke Mister Mist's mane.

"Now, Benny, if you want to feed Hazel, put the sugar on the palm of your hand and hold your hand flat."

Benny followed the farmer's instructions. "Oooh, she tickles," said Benny, yanking his hand away after the horse had taken the sugar cube. Then he quickly gave Mister Mist his sugar, while Seymour gently nudged Hazel out of the way.

## The Missing Letters

Benny did not want to leave the horses, but the others were eager to continue exploring the farm.

Seymour led the way to a long, low building. "This is a shed and junk room," the farmer explained as he pulled open the wooden door and held it for the Aldens.

"Wow!" Henry exclaimed when his eyes had adjusted to the dim light.

Inside was a large wagon. It was old and rusted now, but Seymour told them it had been used as a horse-drawn buggy. The wagon was piled high with old trunks, bundles of yellowed newspapers, and wooden crates filled with glass jars and old rusty tools.

Half the shed held modern farm equipment: tractors, ladders, buckets, hoses, pitchforks, fertilizers, and pesticides. But it was the buggy that interested the Aldens the most.

"How old is it?" Henry wanted to know.

"What's in all those trunks?" asked Benny.

"One question at a time," Seymour advised, laughing. "That buggy dates back to Gideon's time, I dare say. As for what's in those trunks, I suggest

that some rainy day you all have a look."

"Oh, we'd love to do that," Jessie answered for all of them.

"I've rummaged around in one or two of them," Seymour continued. "As far as I can recall, I found some old clothes, some hats, and even some books. Just about all the Curtises are collectors. We never seem to throw anything away."

"Is the secret passageway in this shed?" Benny wanted to know.

"Ah, young man, I was saving the best part for last," Seymour said. "We need to go back up to the house to find the secret passageway."

"Okay," said Benny, racing outside.

***

Once in the house, Seymour led the Aldens downstairs to the basement—a long, low room with stone walls and a dirt floor.

The children looked all around the basement. The only door in any of the walls was one at the top of a short wooden staircase that obviously led to the outside.

"How can there be a secret door?" Henry asked.

"It would have to be made out of this stone that's in the walls, and that would be awfully heavy."

Violet spotted a tall wooden cabinet that stood against one wall near a corner. "Is the door behind this cabinet?" she asked.

Seymour chuckled. "You're pretty darn close!" he answered as he walked over to the cabinet and opened it. There was little inside it besides two flashlights and an old kerosene lamp on the top shelf.

Seymour moved the lamp aside, handed one flashlight to Henry, and switched on the other. Holding it in one hand, he took hold of one shelf, jiggled it slightly, then pushed on it.

To the Aldens' amazement, all the shelves and the back of the cabinet swung backward like a door, revealing a narrow opening. A cold draft blew out at them.

"The secret passageway!" shouted Benny.

# CHAPTER

# The Secret Passageway

The Aldens peered inside the opening. The passageway looked so dark and spooky with cobwebs hanging overhead that Benny was suddenly afraid to step inside, even after Seymour handed him a flashlight.

"Come on, Benny. This is one of the things you came all this way to see," Seymour said.

"I'll go after Henry," Benny said in a quavery voice.

Henry had to bend down to go through the opening. He shone his flashlight against the walls and gave a gasp.

"What's the matter?" asked Benny, who was right behind his brother.

# The Secret Passageway

"It's a...it's just that I thought I saw a person in here," Henry explained, sounding a little sheepish. "Now I see that it's a suit of armor." Henry shone his flashlight all around. He saw not just one but six steel suits of armor, complete with helmets, lining the walls of the narrow passageway.

"Neat," Benny said as he came inside. The others crowded in behind him.

Besides the armor, there were lots of old weapons: knights' swords, a battle-ax, a crossbow, and two big shields.

"Wow!" said Benny. "Did they really fight with all this stuff?"

"No, Benny," said Seymour with a chuckle. "For one thing, not all of it is real equipment from the Middle Ages. This suit, for example, is stage armor. It was used in a play in Boston many years ago. It looks real, but it's much lighter than the other suits."

"Are these swords all real?" asked Henry.

"Yes, Henry, they are indeed. This one is from the fifteenth century," the farmer said, shining his light on it. "And this curved one is from Turkey, and here is a naval cutlass from colonial times here in America." Seymour beamed the flashlight on a short, heavy, curved sword. Then Seymour looked around the passageway and said nothing more for a few moments.

"Is something the matter?" Jessie asked.

"It's strange, but I can't find Gideon's officer's saber from the Civil War. It was down here the last time I was."

Jessie and Henry exchanged glances. "You don't think it was stolen, do you?" Henry asked.

The farmer scratched his head. "I don't know what to think. I'd find it hard to believe a burglar would know how to get inside this secret passageway. It's too well hidden. It was built before the Civil War to help runaway slaves escape north. After the Civil War, my ancestor, Gideon, used this passageway to store his sword and armor collection. His collection has been down here ever since, pretty much just the way you see it, though my children and grandchildren have sometimes borrowed some of the armor to use as Halloween costumes."

"Maybe someone borrowed that Civil War sword

for a costume," Jessie suggested hopefully.

Seymour sighed. "I hope so. I must ask Rose if she knows anything about it."

Violet shone her flashlight on the dirt floor to look for clues. But there weren't any, just lots of indistinguishable footprints.

By now the Aldens and Seymour were at the end of the passageway. Seymour shone his light on the wooden trapdoor above them. "That door goes right into the barn," he said. "When we go through it, we'll be right next to Elvira's stall."

Jessie giggled. "Won't she be surprised."

Seymour fetched the ladder that was resting behind one of the suits of armor.

"Want to go out this way?" he asked.

"Sure, why not," Jessie answered for all of them.

Henry was the first one up the ladder.

"Just push the door out," Seymour advised Henry.

"It's heavy," Henry answered, panting.

"I know," said Seymour. "It's part of the floor. I never go out this way because I'm getting too old to fool with that heavy trapdoor."

"I know what you mean," Henry said, huffing. "Aha, finally it's out!" Henry climbed out into the barn. Elvira came over to greet him.

"Your goat is here, Jessie," Henry called into the passageway.

When they were all in the barn, Seymour lowered the trapdoor, then scattered straw to conceal it. Then the Aldens insisted on helping Seymour with the animals. They brought the horses in from the pasture and fed them oats. The cows got hay that Henry pitched into their stall.

The sun was low in the sky when the Aldens walked back to the house with Seymour. Flocks of geese flew overhead, forming a pattern that looked like the letter V.

As soon as they were in the house, Seymour and the Aldens lost no time asking Rose if she had seen Gideon's sword.

"No, I haven't," Rose said, wiping her hands on her blue-and-white-checked apron. "I haven't been in that passageway in months."

"Neither have I." Seymour was scratching his head. He sighed heavily. "You don't know of anyone borrowing that sword for a Halloween costume, or some such getup?"

Rose frowned. "Well, no. I don't remember telling anyone they could borrow a costume this year."

The Aldens looked at one another. "Do you think someone might have borrowed that sword without telling you?" Jessie asked gently.

Seymour sighed and looked at his wife. "It's possible," he said, almost as if he were trying to convince himself. "I mean, we certainly don't keep things under lock and key here. We've never had to."

"That's true," Rose agreed. "We've never had to—until now."

# Veronica

That evening, after an early dinner, the four Alden children met in Jessie and Violet's room.

"We just have to help Seymour and Rose solve this mystery," Violet was saying as she leaned back against two of the lacy white pillows piled on the bed.

"All this is very upsetting for them," Henry agreed, "especially since they think the burglar may be someone who works for them."

"I hope it's not," Violet said.

"I hope not too," said Henry. "But a burglar who works here would be easier to catch."

"True," Jessie agreed. She pulled a notebook and pencil out of her blue duffel bag. "We should make

42

a list of all the people who work on this farm and who know about the entrances to the passageway."

"Well, there's Jeff and Mike," Violet said, "the ones we met at lunch."

"The ones who've been working on the farm since they were in high school." Jessie was busy scribbling in her notebook.

"Mike seemed awfully quiet once the robberies were mentioned," Violet remarked.

"I don't think Mike and Jeff are really suspects," Henry said.

"What makes you so sure?" Jessie said, holding her pencil poised over her notebook.

"Seymour has known them too long, and nothing has ever been taken from the farm before," Henry answered.

"That's true." Jessie tapped her pencil on her notepad.

"Well, that leaves Veronica and Martin, the two high school kids who just started working on the farm this year," Violet said.

"The ones we haven't seen yet," Jessie said, looking up from her notebook.

"We should ask Seymour if we can meet them tomorrow," Henry said.

"And we should also try to find Benny's ghost. Right, Benny?" Jessie looked over at her brother, only to find that Benny had fallen sound asleep and was snoring gently.

"It's been a long day," Jessie whispered. Henry nodded as he carefully picked up Benny to carry him off to bed.

*** 

The next morning the Aldens woke up just before sunrise. "It was the rooster," Benny told Grandfather at breakfast. "It was the rooster that got me up so early."

"That's his job," Grandfather said, laughing.

As soon as breakfast was over, Henry, Jessie, Violet, and Benny hurried to the barn to help Seymour feed the animals.

They watched carefully as Seymour milked the cows. "I do it the old-fashioned way," he said as he sat on a pail beside one of his cows and began pulling at her teats. Milk squirted into another pail under the cow.

"Many farmers use milking machines now," Seymour explained. "But I don't have enough cows for a machine. It's easier for me to milk them this way."

"I'd like to try to milk a cow before I leave," Henry said.

"Oh, I trust you'll have the chance," said Seymour, chuckling. "But right now, if you like, you can brush down the horses."

"Sure," said Henry, grabbing a brush.

"Hey, that's my job." A tall, thin girl with shiny brown hair tied back in a ponytail strode into the barn. "I always brush the horses," she said haughtily. "They're used to me." The girl wore blue jeans, a red-and-black-plaid wool jacket, riding boots, and a red bandanna around her neck. Her blue eyes flashed as she glared at Henry.

"Now, Veronica," Seymour said gently. "It's good for the horses to have other folks brushing them down once in a while. They need to get used to other people."

Veronica continued to glare at the Aldens as Seymour introduced them to her.

"Are you used to horses?" she asked Henry, who was still holding the brush. "Do you know how to groom them properly?"

"Well, not really," Henry was forced to admit.

Veronica rolled her eyes.

"That's all right, son," said Seymour. "Veronica or I can teach you all you need to know. Isn't that right, Veronica?"

Veronica sighed heavily. "How long will you be staying here?" she asked.

"About a week or two," Jessie answered for all of them.

"Well, that's hardly worth taking the time to teach you," Veronica remarked.

"Now, Veronica," Seymour spoke sharply, "the Aldens are my guests. They've already been a big help to me, and I will thank you to treat them politely. If you don't feel like showing them what needs to be done, then I'll teach them myself."

Veronica scowled. "I'll show them," she said sullenly.

Veronica and the Aldens spent the next hour together feeding, grooming, and brushing the horses, while Seymour mended some fences outside. Veronica showed the Aldens what had to be done by doing most of the work herself, while they watched.

"Now, I don't want you riding Hazel or Mister Mist without my permission," Veronica was saying as she brushed Mister Mist. "They're not used to strangers. They only like it when I handle them. Seymour says I'm the best rider on this farm—the best rider in this whole town, in fact."

"We wouldn't ride them without asking anyone," Jessie said.

"Good."

Henry cleared his throat. "It's a shame about those robberies, isn't it?"

Veronica stiffened. "What robberies are you talking about?"

"You know, the robberies on this farm," Jessie said. "Someone stole Seymour's stamp collection and some old letters written more than a hundred years ago."

Veronica frowned. "No one told me," she said. "When did this happen?"

"A few days ago," Henry answered. "At least that's when Seymour noticed that the stamp collection and letters were missing."

"He's missing a sword too. A sword from the Civil War," Benny added before he noticed Jessie's face warning him to keep quiet.

Veronica looked puzzled. "You mean someone stole a sword out of that musty old passageway?"

Henry nodded.

"I don't like to hear that there were burglars near the barn because that means the horses could be in danger," Veronica said as she fluffed up Mister Mist's mane.

"From what Seymour said, these burglars are after antiques, not animals," Henry pointed out.

"Well, still, I worry. If anything happened to these horses, I don't know what I'd do."

"You seem to care for these horses very much," Violet said, softening a little toward Veronica.

"Well, of course. Who wouldn't?" Veronica exclaimed. Then she frowned suddenly and turned away from the Aldens to hang the grooming brushes back on the wall. "I have to go home now.

I mostly just help with the horses now that the picking season is over."

"Have you been working here long?" Henry wanted to know.

"Have you been here long enough to see the ghost?" Benny asked.

"No and no." Veronica actually smiled for the first time that morning. "I began working for Seymour this fall because he needed the extra help, but I've known Rose and Seymour all my life, practically. I live just down the road."

"Why have you never seen the ghost if you live near here?" Benny asked.

"Well, to tell you the truth," Veronica began in a superior tone of voice, "I don't believe in ghosts. Maybe that's why I've never seen it." With that, Veronica spun around and walked out of the barn before the Aldens could say anything more.

"Boy, is she rude," Jessie muttered.

"She wasn't so bad, once we got her to talk more," Violet remarked.

"But she's such a show-off." Jessie was almost sputtering. "She hardly let us touch her precious horses, and they're not even her horses, really. And did you see the way she acted when we mentioned those robberies?"

"Yeah, she looked kind of uncomfortable. And then she told us she'd never heard about them," Henry said.

"We'll have to watch her," Jessie said.

"We should watch everybody," Henry advised.

"Now, don't you mind Veronica too much," Seymour told the Aldens when he walked back into the barn. "She acts all high and mighty, especially when it comes to the horses, but she's all right."

Jessie was not convinced.

"Seymour?" Benny began. "You believe in the ghost, don't you?"

"Benny, to tell you the truth, I've never actually seen it. But people have noticed signs."

"What kind of signs?" Benny sounded eager.

Seymour chose his words carefully. "Well, Benny, some of the farmworkers say they've heard things."

Benny nodded. "Grandfather told us about that," he said.

"And some say they've actually seen markings on the trunks of the apple trees. Markings carved by a knife of some sort," Seymour continued. "They think those markings are the work of the ghost because no one else would mark those trees up."

Benny's eyes were very round.

"Do you believe a ghost made those markings?" Violet asked.

Seymour's eyes twinkled. "Well, now that you mention it, there is another explanation for these markings," he answered.

"There is?" Benny couldn't believe it.

Seymour nodded. "When my children were little, they used to make carvings in those trees with their penknives. But when I caught them doing that, I made them stop."

"So, those markings are pretty old, then," Henry remarked.

"Yes, most of them are, but Jeff told me he's been seeing some new ones. He thinks it's the work of kids in the neighborhood."

"It could be the work of the ghost," Benny said firmly.

"Could be," Seymour said. "That's what a lot of people think."

"This we have to see!" Henry exclaimed.

# Signs in the Orchard

Before long, the Aldens were walking through thick rows of apple trees. The wind swirled red and yellow leaves around them.

"It's pretty here," Violet observed.

"It is," Benny agreed. "But how are we ever going to hear the ghost with all this wind?"

Henry shook his head and stopped before a group of apple trees with thicker trunks. "These look like the oldest trees in the orchard," he said. "I think this is where Seymour said some markings would be."

Indeed, when the Aldens bent down they could see weathered drawings carved into the bark. There was an X, an O, and a symbol that Henry

thought looked like a rough drawing of a sword.

"Maybe the O is really an apple," Violet suggested.

"What does the X stand for?" Benny wanted to know.

Henry shrugged. "Beats me," he said. "Remember, this was part of a game Seymour's children used to play."

"Let's see if we can't find the newer markings," Jessie suggested. "These carvings are pretty faded."

The Aldens walked alongside the trees, crunching fallen leaves beneath their sneakers. Benny gathered a pile of the leaves in his arms and threw them at Violet. Violet threw some leaves back at Benny. Before long, masses of leaves whirled through the air.

"Looks like you're having fun," a voice said.

The Aldens turned to face a tall blond boy who stood grinning at them. "I was just pruning some of these apple trees," the boy explained as he pointed to the large power saw by his feet. "I work in this orchard part-time after school."

"Are you Martin?" Jessie asked.

The boy nodded. "I am," he said. "And you must

be the Aldens. Seymour told me you'd be visiting. I'm pleased to meet you."

"We're pleased to meet you too," Jessie said for all of them.

"We're looking at these markings on the tree trunks," Benny informed Martin. "Do you know about them?"

"Oh, those," Martin said, laughing. "I think they must have been part of a game the Curtis children used to play."

Benny looked disappointed.

"Are there any other markings like this?" Violet asked.

"I haven't seen any," Martin answered. "But then again, I haven't been looking."

"What do you know about the ghost?" Benny asked Martin.

Martin laughed. "Well, I've heard some rustling in the trees, but I think it's the sound of an animal, not a ghost."

"You've never seen the ghost?" Benny asked.

"No, I don't think I have," Martin answered. "But you know, in most of the ghost stories I've read, the ghost never actually appears."

"It doesn't?" Benny's eyes were as round as saucers.

"No." Martin sounded very sure. "The room, or the area where the ghost is supposed to appear, just gets colder. And lights flicker, that kind of stuff. People sense a ghost is around, but no one ever actually sees it."

"I never thought of it that way." Benny sounded much happier. He walked farther into the orchard, and the others followed, including Martin.

Henry was the first to see two markings scratched into the bark of one tree. "These markings look newer!" he exclaimed.

"Why do you think so?" Violet asked as she bent down to look at them more carefully.

"They don't look as weathered," Henry answered. "So it's easier to make out what they are."

"It's true," Jessie agreed. She sat on the ground near Henry. "Here's a drawing of a sword with a curved blade."

"That's interesting," Henry said. "Do you think this is still part of the game?"

"It could be a message or signal for someone," Violet suggested.

Jessie's eyes lit up. "I wonder if the sword that's missing has a curved blade."

"Maybe it's the ghost of Joshua saying he wants that sword," Benny pointed out.

"Maybe," Martin said. "But I'll bet it's a signal for someone who's alive today, maybe the burglars who take antiques." He sounded as excited as Jessie.

"Yes," Henry agreed. "The message could be that the coast is clear to take a sword with a curved blade."

"We should tell Seymour right away," Jessie said. Benny had already turned around to go back to the farmhouse.

The Aldens and Martin had not gotten too far when Veronica stepped out from behind a tree and walked directly into their path.

"Martin, I've been looking all over for you." She sounded angry.

"Oh, hi, Veronica," Martin said, blushing a little.

"Why weren't you over by the tree where you

said you would be? Do you know how long it's taken me to find you?"

"Well Veronica, I—"

Veronica put her hands on her hips. "I'm sure you have a good excuse, as always," she interrupted.

"Veronica, I was helping the Aldens find some markings on the trees. We think these markings might be a clue—you know, for those burglaries."

"Oh." Veronica looked somewhat interested. "Why don't we take a walk and you can tell me all about it," Veronica suggested, locking her arm through Martin's.

"So long," Martin said, nodding to the Aldens. He looked sorry to be saying good-bye to them. Veronica firmly led Martin away without a word to the Aldens.

"I can't believe someone as nice as Martin is going out with Veronica," Jessie muttered as the four walked quickly in the other direction—toward the farmhouse.

"She is so rude to us," Violet complained. "Did you see how she acted like we weren't even there?"

"She probably wishes we weren't around," Jessie

remarked. "If it weren't for us, Martin would have been waiting for her by the tree."

"Yeah," Benny agreed.

"You know," Henry began, "I wonder how much of our conversation she overheard. I wonder how long she was behind that tree."

"Do you think she might have been spying on us?" Violet wondered.

"That is just what I was thinking," Henry admitted.

\*\*\*

"Well, did you see the markings?" Seymour wanted to know as soon as the Aldens walked in the door of the farmhouse.

"We sure did," Jessie said.

"We saw two kinds," Benny added. "Old ones and new ones. And I bet the new ones were drawn by the ghost."

"Where were these new markings, exactly?" Seymour wanted to know.

"Near the horse's pasture," Violet answered.

"We saw a drawing of a sword with a curved blade on one of the trees. It didn't look as old and faded as the others," Henry explained.

"That's odd," Seymour said, scratching his chin. "The missing sword has a curved blade."

"We thought it might," Henry said, looking excited. "We think it might be a signal."

"A signal for the burglar," Seymour said, frowning. "I'd like to see this marking."

"We'll lead the way," Henry said.

Before Seymour and the Aldens could get out the door, they heard Grandfather calling them from the living room. "Look at this!" Grandfather was almost shouting. The Aldens rushed into the living room ahead of Seymour.

They found their grandfather seated in an old armchair by the window, rustling the newspaper, which lay open on his lap.

"Take a look at this story," Grandfather said as he handed the paper to Henry.

"'Memories of Yesteryear.'" Henry read the headline aloud while the others peered over his shoulder—all but Benny, who was too short.

"'Today's column features a letter that has much to tell us about what life was like in Chassell in the horse-and-buggy days,'" Henry continued reading. Then he gasped.

"What, what's the matter?" Benny cried.

"This letter is addressed to Joshua Curtis," Henry said, lowering the paper so Benny could see it.

"Wow, it was written in 1857," Violet said, looking over Benny's shoulder.

Seymour put on his spectacles and took a closer look at the paper. "Just as I thought," he said grimly. "That's one of Gideon's letters to Joshua. It's also one of the letters that was stolen from my desk."

Henry looked puzzled. "Why did Gideon have a letter addressed to Joshua? Wouldn't Joshua have that letter?"

"Good question," Seymour said. "Gideon made copies of every letter he sent. That's why there's so much correspondence in this house."

"I can't believe that's one of the stolen letters!" Rose said.

"It is," Seymour said, a little gruffly. "It's the letter where Gideon is inviting Joshua to come up for a visit."

"I don't think I ever read that letter," Rose said slowly.

"James, why don't you read that letter aloud?" Seymour suggested.

Grandfather cleared his throat and read:

15 October 1857

Dear Cousin Joshua,

I regret to have taken so long to answer your letter dated August third. We have been busy here planting & gathering this year's crop of apples & corn. It is hard to believe that winter approaches as it has been very warm this October.

Sybil is preparing for the winter holidays, & we are hoping you may join us. I know the trip from Virginia is long, but we could arrange to meet you at the train station & bring you to our farm.

I know we must discuss this matter of dividing my father's sword & armor collection. I have now read his will &

# Signs in the Orchard

diary & see that he wanted me to inherit it. We can discuss this further when I see you.

Sybil, the children & I so hope you can visit & we await your response.

Your cousin, Gideon

"Does the paper say anything about where they found this letter?" Violet asked.

"Yes, it does," Henry answered. "The letter was sent to them by a Mrs. Louise Hathaway, head librarian for the Chassell Public Library."

"I wonder where Louise found that letter," Rose remarked. "We know her. She would never steal anything from anyone."

"We should probably pay a visit to the local library tomorrow," Henry offered. "We can ask her in person."

"Oh, would you?" Seymour sounded grateful. "I can't leave the farm tomorrow because I want to supervise the pruning."

"We'd be glad to go to the library," Jessie said. "Maybe we can find more clues there."

**65**

# CHAPTER 7

# A Stranger in the Library

The Aldens were up early the next morning. They helped feed the animals and ate a quick breakfast. Then they borrowed some old bicycles that were in the shed and rode into Chassell.

The library was in a large white clapboard house that was painted white and had green shutters. The Aldens climbed up the brick staircase and entered a large, comfortable reading room.

Luckily Mrs. Hathaway was one of the librarians on duty. She towered over the Aldens, even Henry, when she stood.

"We're guests of the Curtises," Henry began, looking up at the librarian, who was staring at him very closely.

"Yes."

"Well, we were curious about the old letter reprinted in the paper. The paper said that was your letter—I mean, that the letter belonged to you."

Mrs. Hathaway nodded.

"We were just wondering where you found that letter. I mean, did you know it was stolen property?" Henry continued.

Mrs. Hathaway scowled. "Now, young man, I bought that letter at a respectable antique shop on the outskirts of town—a shop I am sure would not be selling stolen property."

"But there have been other antiques stolen in town recently," Jessie persisted.

Mrs. Hathaway nodded a bit impatiently. "Yes, young lady, I am aware of that. But I am sure this shop would not be selling stolen goods, as I've said before."

"Did you buy any other letters with it?" Jessie wanted to know.

"No, I did not, not this time, though I have bought old letters and diaries from that shop in the past. I collect articles on the town's early history for the library."

"Are the letters you've bought from this shop in the library?" Jessie asked eagerly.

"They most certainly are. You'll find them on display in the small reading room to the right," said Mrs. Hathaway, pointing. "Now may I ask why you think that letter in the paper was stolen?"

The Aldens looked at one another. "That letter belonged to Mr. Curtis," Benny blurted out. "He's had a bunch of letters and other things stolen from his house."

Mrs. Hathaway looked surprised, even a little embarrassed. "Goodness, I had no idea."

Jessie told Mrs. Hathaway about the robberies on the farm. When she was finished, Mrs. Hathaway shook her head. "Poor Seymour. He certainly has been having trouble. I suppose it makes sense that letter belongs to him, since it does concern one of his ancestors. I must return it to him." Mrs. Hathaway led the Aldens to the display case and unlocked it.

"Here are the other old letters that belong to the

library. Many were donated or purchased a long time ago, so I doubt they belong to Seymour."

Mrs. Hathaway carefully took Joshua's letter out of the display case. "I will go out to the farm myself to return this to Seymour," she told the Aldens. "Please tell him I'll visit tonight when I'm off duty."

Henry nodded. "We'll tell him."

"I must also let the antique store know about this," Mrs. Hathaway said.

"We'd like to talk to this antique dealer too," Henry said.

"That's probably a good idea," Mrs. Hathaway remarked. "Seymour is indeed lucky to have you as houseguests."

"While we're here," Violet began shyly, "would it be all right if we looked through these other old letters? We would love to read more about Gideon's time." She nodded in the direction of the display case.

"Well, I suppose you could, if you're very careful with them," the librarian answered, looking suspiciously at Benny.

"We will be," Henry assured her.

With the librarian's permission, the Aldens

moved the contents of the display case to a reading table so they could study the old maps and letters more closely.

"Look, here's the Curtis farm," Henry said, pointing at an old map. "They sure had a lot of land in the old days," he said. "Look, they had all the land that now belongs to the Browns—you know, the farm we passed on the way to town."

"That's interesting," Jessie said thoughtfully. "Maybe they had to sell some of their land off because they needed the money."

"Look at this. Here's an old drawing of Chassell in 1890. It looks pretty much the same," Violet remarked as she carefully handed the drawing to Henry.

"Yeah, except you don't see too many horse-drawn carts in the street now," Henry joked. "Also, the streets weren't paved then."

"Here's a picture of the old library when it was a house with a family in it." Violet handed the yellowed photograph to Jessie.

"Look, there are some Curtises in the picture," Violet said, pointing at the caption.

# A Stranger in the Library

The Aldens were so intent on their research, none of them noticed the tall man with blond hair and a beard who approached their table. He had been listening to their conversation ever since they had begun talking to the librarian. Finally he cleared his throat.

Violet looked up, startled. "Pardon me," the man said. "I'm Blake Ambrose."

The Aldens nodded politely. The name was not familiar to them.

"I'm the author of numerous mysteries and horror stories," the man continued, looking a little disappointed that the Aldens had never heard of him. "My newest book is set in a small nineteenth-century New England village, much like Chassell."

The Aldens nodded politely. "Is that why you're in this library?" Benny wanted to know.

"Well, yes," the author answered. He acted as if Benny had asked a very stupid question. "I'm doing some research on this town. And I, uh, couldn't help overhearing your earlier conversation with Mrs. Hathaway. I could perhaps help you in your research. You see, I am an expert on early American

history." Mr. Ambrose stood up very straight as he said this.

Jessie looked at him a little suspiciously but did not say anything.

"How long have you been staying with the Curtises?" Mr. Ambrose wanted to know.

"Not that long," Violet answered vaguely. "Do you know them?"

"The Curtises are an old New England family. I've been reading about them here. Are you going to be staying out at their orchard a long time?"

"A couple of weeks," Henry answered.

"Have you discovered any skeletons in the closet?" the author joked.

"What?" Benny looked puzzled.

"You know, old family secrets."

"Well, we're trying to find out more about what life was like in the ghost's time," Benny answered, not noticing Jessie's warning look.

"Oh, you mean Joshua," the author replied with a wink.

"You know about Joshua?" Jessie sounded surprised.

"I certainly do," the author replied. "The story of Joshua and his disappearance is an interesting part of the history of this town."

"Do you know what happened to Joshua?" Benny asked.

"I'm working on finding out," the author replied.

"We are too," Benny said, looking at the stack of yellowed letters on the desk in front of him. "And so far we haven't had much luck."

"We'll let you know if we have any questions about anything," Henry told Mr. Ambrose, who was peering at a letter over Henry's shoulder.

"Good day," the author said as he walked away.

"Maybe we should have been a little friendlier to him," Violet whispered when the author had disappeared into the reference section.

"I think he was kind of nosy," Henry said. "I didn't like him looking over my shoulder like that."

"Yeah, I didn't really trust him, either," Jessie said. "That's why I didn't want you telling him too much, Benny."

"I don't think I told him anything he didn't know already," Benny pointed out.

"I don't think you did," Jessie said reassuringly.

"He may have only been trying to help us," Violet said as she pulled her hair back into a ponytail and fastened it with a lavender ribbon.

Henry shrugged. "It sounds like he spends a lot of time in the library. If we have any questions, we know where to find him."

The Aldens spent the rest of the morning reading old letters and looking at maps and photographs, but they could find no further clues to the mystery of Joshua's disappearance.

"We'd better go to the antique store soon," Henry said finally, looking at his watch. "It's going to take us a while to get there."

"Can't we have lunch first?" Benny suggested. "I'm starving."

"Good idea," Jessie said approvingly.

Before they left, Mrs. Hathaway gave the Aldens detailed directions on how to find the antique store. "It's really a barn with a lot of old furniture and other odds and ends in it," she said. "And it's just a little ways outside of Chassell on Old Post Road, the road you took from Seymour's farm. You can't miss it."

"Do you know where we might go for lunch?" Jessie asked as the Aldens were on their way out the door.

"The Doughnut Shop across the street sells delicious sandwiches as well as homemade pies, cakes, and, of course, doughnuts."

"Let's go!" Benny almost shouted.

\*\*\*

When the Aldens entered the Doughnut Shop, they saw Blake Ambrose seated at a table reading a newspaper.

"That's funny. I never saw him leave the library," Henry remarked.

Jessie shrugged. "We weren't looking at the door the whole time," she reminded Henry.

The author looked up and waved as a waitress led the Aldens past his table, but he seemed too absorbed in his newspaper to want to talk.

"Let's not take too long with lunch," Henry warned as the Aldens sat in a booth by the window. "We want to have plenty of time at the antique shop and still get home before dark."

"Can't we at least have dessert?" Benny pleaded,

eyeing a plate of homemade chocolate doughnuts behind the counter.

"Why don't we have lunch here and then take some doughnuts to go," Jessie suggested.

"Okay," Benny reluctantly agreed.

While the Aldens were wolfing down their bacon, lettuce, and tomato sandwiches, Martin and Veronica walked into the Doughnut Shop. Martin smiled and waved to the Aldens, but Veronica ignored them. To their surprise, Veronica did wave to Blake Ambrose, who nodded and smiled at her.

"How do they know each other?" Henry wondered.

"Yeah, that's strange," Jessie agreed. "Maybe we can ask Martin." Jessie was about to wave Martin over to their table, but he was busy buying two jelly doughnuts at the counter. He quickly paid for them and walked out of the store with Veronica at his heels.

"Very strange," Violet said. "Maybe we should ask Mr. Ambrose how he knows Veronica."

But when they turned around to look at Blake Ambrose, the author had vanished.

"How did we miss him?" Henry was surprised. "He was just here."

Jessie looked over at the author's table. The remains of his tuna sandwich lay on his plate. The newspaper he had been reading was neatly folded beside his place setting, and he had left money on the table to pay for his meal.

"He sure comes and goes quickly," Jessie remarked. "I think it's interesting that Veronica knows him. That may be an important clue."

"You mean because Veronica works on the farm?" Violet asked.

Jessie nodded. "Veronica could be giving Blake information about the secret passageway and what's in it."

"That's true," Henry agreed. "But we really don't have any evidence that Blake is involved in these burglaries. All we know is that he's nosy."

"And he knows Veronica," Jessie repeated as she pulled her notebook out of her backpack. She added Blake's name to her list of suspects.

When the Aldens were finished, they paid for their lunch at the counter and bought a bag of assorted doughnuts to go. (Benny made sure they were mostly chocolate ones.) Then they walked back to the library to get their bicycles.

Once on the road, Benny was sure he kept seeing the same large blue car not too far behind them. Henry noticed it, too, and wondered if they were being followed.

By the time the Aldens reached the store, the car had disappeared. They never saw the driver.

## CHAPTER 8

# The Antique Store

"Goodness, I had no idea that letter was stolen. That's dreadful!" the owner of the antique store exclaimed. Mrs. Holmes was a round, short woman with wiry gray hair. "I would never knowingly sell stolen merchandise," she told the Aldens. "I must call the police about this."

"Mrs. Holmes," Jessie said gently, "do you remember who brought the letter in?"

The owner sighed and looked around her store. "I have so many things in here," she said wearily. "It's hard to keep track of who brings in what. I buy most of my things at yard sales and auctions, but I don't believe that's where the letter came from. I wish I could remember more. I really do.

## The Antique Store

And I must apologize to Seymour." Mrs. Holmes was wringing her hands.

"That letter would have come in recently," Henry pointed out.

"Well, we don't know that for sure," Jessie reminded her brother. "Seymour doesn't exactly know when the letters were stolen."

"True," Henry agreed. "But we think it was within the last month or so."

"Seymour is also missing a stamp collection and a sword dating from the Civil War. You don't have anything like that around, do you?" Henry asked.

Mrs. Holmes shook her head. "Good heavens, no. That I'm sure of. I just wish I could remember more about the letter. If you'll give me a few moments, I'll check my files. Perhaps I can find some record there."

"Sure, we'll just look around your store awhile," Violet offered. "You might even remember more while we're here."

"I'll certainly try to," Mrs. Holmes assured her. "I just wish I kept better records of things." The owner vanished behind a large oak desk and started rummaging through some cardboard boxes that served as her filing cabinets.

Henry walked over to a pile of newspapers. Jessie looked at some old glass vases in a cabinet. Violet and Benny went to a corner where there were some old toys: dolls, wooden blocks, and rocking horses.

"These are such old toys," Violet said as she lifted a doll's dress to inspect her petticoat.

"Those are the best kind," the owner muttered. She sat on the floor surrounded by scraps of paper. "Oh, this is useless," she said sadly. "I'm never going to find anything in this mess."

Violet came over to her. "Mrs. Holmes," she began, "do you remember buying the letter from someone?"

The owner nodded and pushed her wire-rimmed glasses on top of her head. "I believe I did. I don't remember buying that letter at a yard sale. I think I would have remembered that."

"Was this person who sold you the letter a woman or a man?" Violet continued.

"A man, I believe," Mrs. Holmes answered.

"Did this man have long blond hair and a beard? Did he say he was an author?" Violet asked.

# The Antique Store

Mrs. Holmes frowned. "No, I don't remember meeting anyone like that. I usually remember faces. That's about all I do remember well."

The Aldens waited while Mrs. Holmes rummaged through a few more cardboard boxes stuffed with papers, but she never found any record of the letter.

"I don't want to keep you here any longer," the owner finally said. "I know Seymour's number. If I find anything, or remember who sold me the letter, I will give you a call. I promise."

"Thanks for all you have done," Jessie said as the Aldens waved good-bye and filed out the door. Once outside, they were surprised to find that the sun was low.

"We should try to get home before dark," Henry warned the others.

"I didn't realize we had been in that store so long," Jessie remarked. "Everything was so old in there, it was almost like being in another century."

The others laughed.

"I wish Mrs. Holmes had been able to remember who brought her the letter," Violet remarked as the Aldens were mounting their bicycles.

"That would have made our job a little easier," Henry remarked as he began to pedal away.

Jessie was about to follow when she noticed a large blue car parked under some trees near the antique store's driveway. The car flashed its lights and began to move toward the Aldens.

"Who is that?" Jessie asked out loud.

The car pulled alongside Jessie, Violet, and Benny. "How about a ride home?" a deep voice asked.

"Mr. Ambrose!" Jessie was so startled she almost shouted.

"What are you doing here?" Benny wanted to know. He was right behind Jessie.

"I was out exploring the area," Mr. Ambrose answered smoothly.

"We don't want a ride home," Benny said firmly.

"It's true," Jessie agreed. "What would we do with our bicycles?"

"I would probably have room for them in my trunk," Mr. Ambrose answered.

"We still don't need a ride." Benny remained firm.

"Were you driving out here to visit the antique store?" Jessie asked. She stood with one foot on the ground, the other on a bicycle pedal.

"Uh, no," Mr. Ambrose answered.

"Have you ever been in this store before?" Jessie persisted.

"I was here once or twice when I first began my research," the author answered. Then he cleared his throat. "Well, if you don't need a ride, I really must be on my way," he added. Before the Aldens could say anything more, the author pulled the car away and sped down the road.

\*\*\*

"You know I saw a big blue car like that following us to the antique store," Benny informed his family when they were back on Seymour's farm. The four were walking their bicycles to the shed to put them away.

"I noticed that car too," Henry remarked. "I'm sure it was Blake's car."

"But why would he want to follow us?" Violet asked as she walked her bicycle beside Henry's.

"Well, if he is involved in these burglaries, he

probably wants to find out how much we know," Henry suggested.

"And he probably doesn't want us to get in his way," Jessie added.

***

That evening, after dinner, Violet and Benny decided to take a walk in the orchard with one of Seymour's flashlights. Benny wanted to hear the ghost for himself, and Violet thought it might be good to keep him company.

It was a windy night, and as Violet waved the flashlight at the scarecrow, it looked like he was waving at them.

"Poor scarecrow," Violet said sadly. "He's probably going to need to be restuffed after this windy night."

"I bet we'll hear the ghost tonight," Benny said eagerly. He walked into the orchard, with Violet at his heels. At that moment, the two heard some whispering and a low call that sounded like a long, drawn-out *boooooo*.

"What's that?" Benny asked.

Violet listened closely.

"Whooooooo...Whooooooo...Whooooooo."

"It could be an owl," Violet answered, but she did not sound very sure. Being out in the orchard after dark was spookier than she had thought.

"No, it's not," Benny said stubbornly.

"How far do you want to go?" Violet asked.

"Not too far," Benny said. His voice was a little quavery as he peered into the dark mass of fruit trees whose branches looked as if they could reach out and grab him. "Are there wolves out here?" Benny wanted to know.

"I don't think so. In fact, I'm sure there aren't."

Just at that moment, Benny and Violet heard a long, low hiss. Benny jumped two feet in the air. "Do you hear that?" he shouted, clutching Violet's arm. "I bet that's a snake."

Violet stopped walking and shone her flashlight on some low bushes behind the trees. Stray leaves were rustling in the wind, making a hissing sound— *pssst, pssst, pssst.* "That might be the whispering sound we're hearing," Violet said hopefully.

"Are you sure?" Benny asked.

"Yes." Violet's voice quavered. She wasn't really

sure, but she wanted Benny to believe she was.

To get their minds off the hissing noise, Violet shone her light, which was getting dimmer, on the trees in front of her. Something she saw made her stop short and stare. "Benny, that marking. It wasn't here the last time we were in the orchard."

"What marking?" Benny rushed over to the tree where the flashlight shone on its bark. In the dim light, he could see a drawing of a helmet, next to the drawing of the sword the Aldens had seen earlier.

"You're right," Benny said. "Do you think the ghost drew this?"

"No, I don't," Violet said. "But I hope it doesn't mean that a helmet is missing from Seymour's collection."

"Oh, I hadn't thought of that," Benny exclaimed. "We'd better check the secret passageway right away." At that moment, the flashlight went out. Violet and Benny could not believe how dark it seemed, even in the moonlight.

# CHAPTER 9

# By the Light of the Moon

"I'm scared," Benny admitted.

Violet gulped. "Take my hand. We're not far from the farm."

Guided by the moonlight, Violet and Benny made their way home, stumbling over rocks and large branches in their path.

"Things sure look different in the dark," Benny muttered as two bats fluttered over them.

"Ugh." Violet shuddered. She let go of Benny's hand and almost dropped her flashlight so she could cover her hair. "I can't stand bats."

Benny and Violet were very happy to see the farmhouse in the distance, lit with a warm light from the lamps in the living room.

# By the Light of the Moon

***

Twenty minutes later, all the Aldens and Seymour were in the secret passageway. Carefully they shone their flashlights on all the suits of armor.

"Oh, no!" Violet groaned. Just as she had feared, one of the helmets was missing.

"That's the most valuable helmet in the collection." Seymour sounded angry. "That thief sure knows what he's doing."

***

That night, before they went to bed, Henry, Jessie, Violet, and Benny met in Jessie and Violet's bedroom. Jessie sat on the large bed, her notebook in hand. "We have to do something before anything else disappears," she said firmly. "At least we have some leads."

Henry nodded. "We suspect Blake Ambrose is involved."

"And someone from the farm must be helping him," Jessie added. "Remember, Seymour told us that only the farmworkers know how to get inside the secret passageway. Someone from the farm must be involved too."

91

"Now we just have to find out who," said Benny. He sat with his legs crossed on Jessie's bed.

"Blake knows Veronica," Violet said. "I wonder if he knows anyone else who could be helping him."

"I think Veronica and Blake are our two most likely suspects," Jessie said. "But we shouldn't forget about Martin, Mike, and Jeff. I think anyone who works in the orchard is a suspect."

"Oh, not Martin," Benny protested. "He's always been so nice to us."

"He has," Henry agreed. "But Martin does spend a lot of time with Veronica. And if she's involved, chances are he may be, also."

"I guess so," Violet said reluctantly.

"What have Mike and Jeff done to make us suspicious?" Jessie asked. She was busy writing in the notebook with a green fountain pen.

"Well, they aren't very likely suspects," Henry admitted. "After all, Seymour has known them a long time, and we haven't caught them behaving suspiciously."

"No, they seem to work very hard," Jessie remarked. "Still, if we really want to find out

what's going on, we should probably observe them as well."

The others nodded.

"Veronica and Martin are usually together, so it shouldn't be too hard to keep track of them," Jessie added. "Why don't Violet and I watch Martin and Veronica, and you two can observe Mike and Jeff," she said to Henry.

"That's fine with me," said Henry. "I don't want to deal with Veronica. It shouldn't be too hard to keep an eye on Mike and Jeff. They're usually in the orchard pruning trees."

"Who's going to watch Blake Ambrose?" Benny wanted to know.

"If he is working with someone from the farm, we might as well wait and have one of the workers lead us to him," Jessie said.

"The only problem with this plan is that it could take a long time for us to catch the thief in action," Henry said.

"That's true," Jessie agreed.

"You know, I have an idea," Violet said quietly. The others turned to look at her. "The thieves must be making those markings on the tree late at night. I doubt anyone would try to mark it up during the daytime."

"True," Henry agreed.

"So," Violet continued, "why don't we camp out in the orchard late at night near that tree and see what happens."

Benny made a face.

"We'll take lots of flashlights this time," Violet said, looking at Benny. "And extra batteries."

"And extra sweaters and maybe blankets," added Jessie.

"It'll be too cold to camp out for the night," Henry said. "It's too bad we don't have a tent or something."

"A tent would be too noticeable," Jessie remarked.

"We should probably plan to do this tomorrow night," Henry said.

The others agreed.

\*\*\*

The following day, Jessie and Violet tried to keep track of Veronica and Martin. Henry and Benny found many excuses to go into the orchard to help Mike and Jeff. No one noticed anything suspicious.

That night after dinner, the Aldens waited until everyone had gone to bed before creeping out to the orchard. After much discussion, they had decided not to tell Grandfather or Seymour of their plan. They knew Grandfather would worry, even though he trusted them to take care of themselves. And they were afraid Seymour would forbid them from going.

Tonight the moon was very full and low in the sky. "That's a Hunter's Moon," Henry said. "It usually comes out in the middle of November."

"It seems brighter out here than it was last night," Benny remarked.

"There aren't as many clouds," Violet observed. "But it's a lot colder."

"I'll say," Benny agreed as he stamped his feet to keep warm. He could see his breath in the cold night air. Violet pulled up the hood of her purple parka. Jessie rubbed her hands together.

"We won't get as cold if we keep moving," Henry suggested as he led the way into the orchard.

# By the Light of the Moon

As the Aldens walked past the scarecrow, they noticed he had fallen over and now lay in a crumpled heap on the ground. Benny noticed his clothes were missing.

"The farm probably doesn't even need a scarecrow this time of year," Jessie said. "Not much is growing."

"Once we're in the orchard, we should probably turn off our flashlights," Henry suggested. "We don't want to attract too much attention."

"But with all these trees around, it's hard to see," Benny pointed out.

"We'll guide you, if you need the help," Henry assured him as Benny obediently turned off his light.

"Don't those tree branches look like claws in the moonlight?" Benny pointed out.

"Oooh, they do," Jessie agreed, shuddering a little. "And what's that noise?"

"What noise?" Benny wanted to know.

"Sssh."

The four Aldens heard the sounds of twigs snapping, then a long, drawn-out, "Whooooooo."

"That's that owl we heard last night," Violet said.

"Whooooo. Whoooooo. Whoooooo."

"That doesn't sound like an owl," Jessie whispered to Violet.

At that moment, a scarecrow came out of the trees and appeared before the Aldens, waving his arms in the moonlight.

"Aaaagh!" Benny shrieked.

# CHAPTER 10

# Joshua's Ghost

"It's the ghost. It's Joshua!" Benny couldn't stop shrieking.

Just as suddenly as he appeared, the ghost vanished—with Henry chasing after him.

"Benny, Benny, calm down," Jessie said soothingly. She hugged Benny to her, while Violet buried her face in Jessie's arm.

"That was so scary," Violet groaned.

"I know it was," Jessie agreed. "I just hope Henry's okay."

"Do you think the ghost will try to hurt him?" Benny asked, looking very serious.

Jessie shook her head. "Benny, I don't think that was really a ghost."

A few minutes later, Henry appeared, looking discouraged. "He was too fast for me. He got away."

"You mean he vanished into the air," Benny said. He knew that was what ghosts did.

"No, he just ran too fast," Henry said as he turned on his flashlight. "But if we follow his path, maybe we can find some clues."

"Clues?" Benny asked.

"Yeah, like footprints or something," Henry said. He walked to the spot where the ghost had been and carefully studied the ground under his flashlight.

"But ghosts don't leave footprints," Benny protested.

"This one did," Henry called. "Look here."

In the ground in front of Henry were a set of extremely large footprints, much larger than Henry's.

"The man sure has big feet," Jessie remarked.

"And I think he wears hiking boots," Violet said as she beamed her flashlight on one of the footprints.

"Who do we know around here with feet that big and hiking boots?" Henry asked.

"Not Mike!" Violet sounded shocked.

Henry nodded.

***

The following day, Henry, Jessie, Violet, and Benny were up early. They had not wanted to wake the others when they came in the night before. The first thing they did was talk to Seymour. They found him in the barn feeding the animals before breakfast.

"You did what? You went out after dark—alone— to try to catch a burglar?" Seymour did not sound happy. "You're lucky you didn't get hurt."

When Seymour had heard the whole story, he shook his head sadly. "I can't believe it's really Mike. I don't understand why he was trying to scare you like that, unless, as you say, he was trying to get you off his trail."

"I suppose it's possible it could be someone else with big feet and hiking boots," Jessie suggested.

"Let's hope so," Seymour said. "But the first thing we need to do is talk to Mike."

On their way out of the barn, Henry spotted something on the ground, under a bush. When he walked over, he saw it was a pile of clothing—the scarecrow's clothing.

"Come here," he called to the others. Henry picked up the large flannel shirt, the denim pants, and the black felt hat. "These are the clothes the scarecrow had on last night," Henry said, handing them to Seymour.

"I might as well take these back to the house," Seymour said. He sniffed the collar of the shirt. "That musky smell—do you recognize it?" he asked the Aldens.

"Sort of," said Jessie, wrinkling her nose. "But I can't place it."

"It's an aftershave Mike sometimes wears," Seymour said sadly.

***

Two hours later, the Aldens and Seymour found Mike in the orchard raking.

"I need to talk to you," Seymour told Mike. "Let's go up to the house." When Mike saw all the Aldens around Seymour, he turned pale and leaned his rake against the side of the tree.

"I think I know what all this is about," he said.

\*\*\*

"There's no excuse for what I did," Mike said, looking at his hands. He sat at the kitchen table with Seymour, Henry, Jessie, Violet, and Benny.

"So you stole my things," Seymour said. He sounded more hurt than angry. "Mike, you've worked for me all these years. What happened? Did you need money?"

"I did. Rob is very sick. Rob's my son," he added for the Aldens' benefit. "He needs money for a kidney transplant. I guess I was desperate. When that guy approached me, wanting me to help him out, I didn't think. He offered me so much money I couldn't refuse."

"What guy?" Benny asked.

"That guy who's hanging around town pretending to be an author. He told me he met you in the library."

"Blake Ambrose," Benny said.

"Right."

"He's not really an author?" Henry sounded surprised.

Mike shrugged. "I think he's written a couple

of horror stories that have sold well. But he makes most of his money stealing antiques and then selling them off to dealers in New York and Boston."

"So you helped him steal the things from here?" Henry asked.

Mike sighed. "Yes. I didn't steal from any other places. Blake would leave me messages carved on one of the trees. I would just take what he wanted me to. He'd given me a list of all the things he wanted from the farm when we agreed to work together."

"If he did that, why did he need to leave you the messages on the tree?" Benny asked.

"I couldn't take everything at the same time," Mike explained. "Blake wanted me to steal the items one at a time, when he was ready for them. He had an odd way of doing things. He hardly ever wanted us to be seen together."

"And you worked alone. I mean, no one else helped you?" Henry wanted to make sure.

"No, no one else was involved," Mike said. "And Blake told me that if the pieces I took didn't sell, I could get them back. I was keeping track of where the pieces went so I could return them to you, someday, if I ever got the money to buy them back," he said to Seymour.

Seymour nodded sadly. "Mike, you should have told me about Rob. I didn't know. I might have been able to help you some other way."

"I know, Seymour." Mike had tears in his eyes, which he tried to brush away. "As I said, I just wasn't thinking. I was so worried about my son."

"So you know where Seymour's things are?" Henry asked.

Mike nodded. "Most of the letters are with a dealer in Boston. So is the stamp collection. But the sword and helmet are still here in Chassell."

Violet looked puzzled. "How come a local antique store had one of the letters?" she asked.

"That was a slipup," Mike explained. "That letter got mixed in with some things I was taking to a yard sale—not any of the stolen goods, but some things from my house I was selling to help raise money. It was careless of me, I admit. Blake was really mad about that letter, especially after it ended up in the local paper. He almost didn't pay me because of it."

"It's funny Mrs. Holmes didn't remember buying

that letter at a yard sale," Violet remarked.

"Mrs. Holmes is kind of absentminded," Mike said.

"She sure is," Seymour agreed, smiling for the first time all morning, but he was serious again when he turned to Mike. "You know, I'm going to have to call the police," he told his farmhand.

"I know," Mike said.

\*\*\*

The police arrived twenty minutes later. "We're going to need you to write out a full confession," one of the police officers told Mike as he led him outside to the waiting car.

"I will," Mike said. "And I want to do all I can to get Seymour's things."

"The more you cooperate in this investigation, the lighter your sentence will be," the officer said.

\*\*\*

That evening, the old black phone in the living room rang three times before Benny rushed to answer it.

"It's for you, Seymour," Benny called. "It's the police."

Benny waited by the phone hoping to hear some news, but the person on the other end of the line was doing most of the talking. "Yes. Yes," Seymour was saying. "Good. Good. Really. Yes. Okay. Thank you."

Benny hopped on one foot, then the other. "What did they say?" he asked after Seymour hung up the phone.

"Well, thanks to Mike's help, the police caught up with Blake Ambrose just outside of Boston. He's wanted in five other states for burglary—all antiques. He's the one who did all the robberies in Chassell."

"Wow," said Benny.

"Are you getting your things back?" Jessie asked as she came into the kitchen, followed by Henry, Violet, Grandfather, Rose, Veronica, Martin, and Jeff.

"Yes. The police are working on that. Apparently my sword and helmet were in Blake's car, so I can have those right away. It may take longer to get the stamp collection and letters, but the police know where they are. And if the dealer has sold them, he's kept records. In time, I'm sure I'll get everything back."

"Thank goodness," Grandfather said.

"What's going to happen to Mike?" Benny wanted to know.

"Since it's his first offense and he cooperated with the police, he won't have to go to jail," Seymour said. "But he may have to do lots of community service."

Jeff shook his head. "I had no idea Mike was under so much financial pressure. He has been looking worried lately, but he keeps everything to himself, so it's hard to know what's really going on with him."

"If we'd known Mike was so desperate, we would have lent him money," Rose said. "We still can."

"I'm planning to," Seymour said.

"That's kind of you," Jeff said.

"What a story," Veronica commented, shaking her head. "Who would have thought all this was happening in this sleepy old orchard?"

"Veronica," Jessie said, "how did you know Blake Ambrose?"

"Oh, I didn't know him very well," Veronica said.

"I used to see him in the library when I was there getting books for my history paper on the Civil War."

"Did he offer to help you with your research?" Henry asked.

"Yes," Veronica said, laughing. "I remember once he seemed kind of mad because I was taking out some books he said he needed. He sure knew a lot about the Civil War. He told me he was an expert on military history."

"That's probably how he knew so much about my sword and armor collection," Seymour remarked. "It is a relief to have this mystery solved."

"Well, one mystery is solved," Benny said. "But I still want to find out about Joshua's ghost."

Veronica rolled her eyes, but everyone else laughed.

\*\*\*

The next three nights, Benny walked out to the orchard, sometimes alone, sometimes with Henry, Violet, or Jessie. Each night he heard a long, low *boo*. On the third night, Jessie convinced him it was really an owl when her flashlight spotlighted the bird in the tree.

"But what about that hissing sound Violet and I heard?" Benny asked.

"It could have been a snake," Jessie said. "But I bet it was the sound of leaves rustling."

"That's what Violet said." Benny sounded extremely discouraged. "You don't really think there's a ghost, do you?"

"No, I don't," Jessie answered.

Benny looked so crushed that Jessie put her arms around him.

\*\*\*

The following morning, it rained. "Why don't we go to the shed to explore that buggy," Jessie suggested.

"Sure," Benny said. "I'll go."

"Be my guests," Seymour said, chuckling. "Let me know if you find anything interesting."

"There's tons of cool stuff in this buggy," Benny said as he looked through a box that held some old spinning tops, marbles, and a set of wooden blocks with letters and drawings carved into them.

"I bet those blocks are handmade," Jessie said. "Someone must have carved them for his children."

"Do you really think so?" Benny held up a block with the letter *D* carved on one side, and a dog on the other.

"It would have been a great way to teach a little kid the alphabet," Henry remarked. He sat inside the buggy poring over some old letters he had seen in one of the wooden chests.

Jessie and Violet were beside the buggy, carefully trying on old hats and petticoats they had found in the steamer trunk.

Benny blew dust off a marble and then dropped it. It fell inside the buggy. As he bent down to look for it, he noticed a long leather bag near his feet. Part of the bag was under a wooden box. Benny moved the box out of the way so he could pick up the bag.

Henry looked up from his reading. "That's a saddlebag," he told Benny. "People used to put them across a horse's shoulders in front of the saddle while riding, to carry stuff."

"Neat," said Benny. "Let's see what's in it." Benny pulled out a newspaper, very yellowed with age, that practically crumbled to pieces as he set it down. Then he took out an old seed catalog, and finally a letter in a long white envelope. The letter was addressed to Mr. Gideon Curtis!

"This letter has never been opened," Benny said. "Should we read it?"

"Maybe we should let Seymour open it," Henry suggested. "It's addressed to his ancestor."

"Look, it's got a Virginia postmark," Jessie said, looking over Benny's shoulder. The feathers in her hat tickled his nose.

"*Aaa-choo!*"

"A Virginia postmark," Henry said, reaching for the letter. "Maybe it's from Joshua!"

The Aldens lost no time finding Seymour. He was sitting at the kitchen table having a cup of coffee with Grandfather and Rose.

"I never knew there was a saddlebag in that buggy," Seymour said as he opened the letter, which was written in ink. "It *is* from Joshua!"

"What does it say?" Benny was so impatient, he was hopping up and down.

Seymour cleared his throat and began reading:

# The Mystery of the Stolen Sword

Virginia

18 November 1865

Dear Cousin,

It has now been eight years since I last saw you. I have not written because I was still very angry we could never come to an agreement about your father's sword & armor collection & then the war began. I left your house in a huff & it has taken me years to stop being so angry. I regret the time we've lost, when we once so enjoyed each other's company, but so be it. I am writing now to tell you I plan to leave the country. The War has left my house and land in ruins & there is nothing left for me here. I plan to go abroad & hope to settle in Australia.

Cousin, as I will probably never see you again, I write to wish you well. Love to Sybil, Theodore, and Alice.

Faithfully yours, Joshua

"My goodness. And this letter has been in the barn all the time! Gideon never opened it. He must have picked up his mail on horseback one time, put it in his saddlebag, and then forgot about it," Rose suggested.

"It's strange he would have forgotten a letter from Joshua," Seymour said. "Maybe he wasn't the one who picked up the mail."

"He never knew his cousin had forgiven him," Violet said.

"Australia. No wonder no one ever heard from him." Seymour couldn't believe it.

"I guess that means Joshua was never really a ghost," Benny said sadly.

"I'm afraid not, Benny." Seymour shook his head.

"Maybe the ghost isn't really Joshua?" Violet teased.

Benny perked up. "I never thought of that."

Everyone laughed.

# THE BOXCAR CHILDREN ®

BOOK
III 120 III

CREATED BY
GERTRUDE
CHANDLER
WARNER

# THE VAMPIRE
MYSTERY

ILLUSTRATED BY
ROBERT PAPP

# Contents

# CHAPTER 1

# The Greenfield Vampire

"Just this one book please," six-year-old Benny said. He gave *The Legend of the Vampire* to the librarian. On the cover was a picture of a scary man in a dark cape. He had two sharp teeth and bloodred lips.

"Oh, Benny, are you sure that is a good book for you?" asked Jessie. She was twelve and kept an eye on her younger brother. "I could help you pick out another."

"No, I want this one, Jessie," Benny said. "Henry found it in the local author's section."

"It was written by Mr. Charles Hudson," explained Henry. At fourteen, he was the oldest.

"Oh!" exclaimed ten-year-old Violet. "Is that the

author Grandfather told us about this morning?"

"I think it is," Henry said.

Mrs. Skylar, the librarian, smiled at the four Alden children. "Mr. Hudson is a local author who has written many exciting books. *The Legend of the Vampire* is one of his bestselling stories. It's set right here in Greenfield."

Violet shivered. "A vampire in Greenfield?" she asked.

"Vampires aren't real, Violet," Jessie said. She put her arm around her sister's shoulders.

"Are you sure?" asked Benny.

"We're sure," Henry said. "Vampires are not real. They're just part of scary stories that people like to read for fun."

"Not real—like ghosts and monsters under your bed?" asked Benny.

"Yes, exactly like that," Jessie said.

"I like scary stories," Benny said. "They always have mysteries in them!" He opened the book to the first page. "'The cem...cem...'" Benny was just learning how to read.

"Cemetery," Henry helped.

"'The cemetery on...'" Benny scratched his forehead.

Violet looked over his shoulder at the page. "Whittaker Street," she told her little brother.

"'Was...dark...and...'" Benny sounded out the words. He sighed. "It's too hard for me. Can you read it to me, Henry?"

"Sure, Benny," Henry said. "But it's getting late now. We promised to meet Grandfather at eleven o'clock."

Jessie looked at her watch. "You're right, Henry." She handed her library card to Mrs. Skylar and checked out her novel. "Grandfather said that he wanted us to meet an old friend of his."

"Do you have the address where Grandfather wants to meet us?" Violet asked.

Henry patted his pocket. "Yes, I have it," he said. "I don't think it's very far. It's on the east end of town."

"Will we be passing any places to eat on the way?" Benny asked hopefully.

"Oh, Benny!" Jessie laughed. Benny had a big appetite. "How can you possibly be hungry after all those pancakes Mrs. McGregor made for you this morning?"

Mrs. McGregor was the Alden's housekeeper. She was a wonderful cook as well.

Benny patted his growling stomach. "I don't know, Jessie," he said. "I guess that's one mystery I'll never be able to solve!"

The Alden children laughed and hopped onto their bikes. In ten minutes they found 52 Whittaker Street. It was an old, quaint house with a small lawn and a blooming flower garden. Grandfather's car was parked out front. He stood on the pale lavender porch talking to a tall man with white hair and a white mustache.

"What a beautiful house!" Violet exclaimed. She was wearing a pale purple top that matched the color of the porch almost exactly. It was her favorite color.

"Why, thank you," the man said, smiling at Violet.

Grandfather rested his hand on Benny's shoulder. "Mr. Hudson, I would like to introduce you to my family. This is Henry, Jessie, Violet, and Benny."

# The Greenfield Vampire

After their parents died, the Alden children ran away. They lived in an abandoned boxcar in the woods until their grandfather found them. He brought them to live with him in his big, white house in Greenfield.

"We're very pleased to meet you," Jessie said.

"Mr. Hudson?" Violet's face flushed red. "The famous author?"

Mr. Hudson laughed. "I'm not all that famous, you know," he said.

"You *are* famous!" Benny cried. He pulled *The Legend of the Vampire* from his backpack. "Your book was in the library!"

Just then a big, blue car screeched to a halt in front of the house. A young man in a business suit jumped out. He hurried up the sidewalk.

"This is the last time!" he said. He hammered a "For Sale" sign into the lawn. His face was red.

Grandfather looked puzzled.

"Don't mind Josh," Mr. Hudson said. "He is my Realtor, and someone keeps stealing his sign from my front lawn. He's been quite upset by it."

Benny looked at Josh banging away on the

metal sign. "What's a Realtor?" he asked.

"A Realtor is a person who tries to help you sell your home," Jessie explained.

"Let me give Josh a hand." Grandfather went over and held the sign steady while Josh hammered.

"Are you moving away from Greenfield, Mr. Hudson?" Henry asked.

"No. I love Greenfield," Mr. Hudson said. "I don't really even want to sell my home." He sighed and looked up at the pretty house. "I've lived here all my life, but it is too big of a place for one old man to take care of on his own. When the house is sold, I'll move to an apartment on the other side of town."

"You mean *if* the house is ever sold," Josh said, wiping his forehead.

"Now, Josh," Mr. Hudson scolded. "Just because the sign keeps disappearing doesn't mean we can't sell the house."

"No, but the broken flowerpots and the old cemetery out back don't help either."

"Old cemetery?" asked Violet.

"Yes," Mr. Hudson replied. "It's quite historic. Some of Greenfield's first citizens are buried back there. You kids are welcome to go take a look. It's actually very beautiful and peaceful."

"Except when the vampire is prowling," Josh added.

The Aldens were too surprised to speak. Violet's face turned white.

"Don't pay attention to Josh," Mr. Hudson hurriedly said. "He gets overly excited sometimes. The vampire is just an old legend."

"But, you said you saw..." Josh tried to argue.

"Now is not the time or place to discuss this, Josh," Mr. Hudson said, glancing over at the Aldens.

"Let's take a walk out back," Jessie said to her sister and brothers. Benny held tightly to Jessie's hand, and Violet stayed close to Henry's side as the Aldens walked back to see the old cemetery. The grass was neatly cut between the rows of the weatherworn headstones.

"What's a legend, anyway?" asked Benny as the children walked.

"It's an old story that has become famous," Jessie said.

"Like Paul Bunyan and his big blue ox," Henry said. "That story is a legend."

Just then the Aldens heard a loud sound in the quiet cemetery. They stopped walking and stared at each other.

Benny groaned. "I'm sorry. I can't help it," he said. "I'm so hungry my stomach keeps growling."

Henry laughed. "I think your appetite is becoming a legend, Benny."

"I know," Benny said. "Right now I think I could eat more than both Paul Bunyan and his ox!"

Violet bent over to look at an old headstone with a pretty flower carved on its front. "This one is hundreds of years old," she said. "The person buried here died in 1742." As she stood up, something caught her eye at the edge of the cemetery.

"Look!" Violet gripped Henry's arm. "There's someone staring at us over there!"

Henry, Jessie, and Benny turned just in time to see the man. He wore a long, dark coat. When he saw that the children had spotted him, he ducked behind a tree and disappeared into the woods.

Violet shivered. "That was odd," she said.

"Not really, Violet," said Henry. "Maybe he was just taking a walk, the same as we were."

"I'm sure Henry's right," Jessie said. "But let's get back to Grandfather now."

# CHAPTER

2

# An Offer to Help

"What do you think of our little cemetery?" Mr. Hudson asked as the children stepped back onto the porch.

"It is quiet and peaceful," Jessie said. "Just like you said it would be."

Josh was rocking back and forth on a squeaky wooden rocking chair in the corner. He glanced at Jessie then quickly looked away and bit down on his lower lip.

"I sure hope you will all stay for some lunch," said Mr. Hudson.

"Lunch? You bet!" cried Benny. "What are we having?"

"Oh, Benny, that's not polite," Jessie said.

"I'm sorry, Mr. Hudson. I didn't mean to be rude." Benny sniffed the air. "But I can smell something really good."

Mr. Hudson laughed. "It tastes as good as it smells, Benny. That's my famous red clam chowder cooking on the stove. I made a big pot of it, and I have a plate of sandwiches as well."

"Clam chowder!" Benny said. "That's my favorite!"

Jessie and Benny set the table, and Henry and Violet poured tall glasses of lemonade for everyone. The kitchen had wide oak floors and pretty flowered curtains on the windows.

"Your home is so beautiful, Mr. Hudson," Violet said.

"Thank you, Violet." Mr. Hudson filled her bowl with hot soup. "I do hate to sell it. It is filled with so many memories. My parents moved here years ago before I was even born. They hoped that the house would always stay in our family."

"Did you write all your books here, Mr. Hudson?" asked Henry. He took a turkey sandwich and passed the tray to Grandfather.

"Yes, Henry, I did. There's a small room upstairs that looks out over the cemetery and the woods. I started writing stories up there when I was a little boy. I get some of my best ideas when I am looking out that window."

Josh dropped his spoon. "Is that where you were when you saw the vampire?" he said.

Mr. Hudson shook his head. "Now, Josh, I thought we agreed not to talk about such things."

"You agreed. I did not." Josh pushed his chair back from the table. "Until we solve this vampire problem, I don't see how I will be able to sell this house. Mrs. Fairfax says she found blood on her back porch yesterday! Some of the other neighbors have heard strange sounds coming from the cemetery at night. Word is getting around town that the vampire in your book has come to life."

The Alden children looked at each other across the table. Benny sat very still, the soupspoon frozen at his lips.

"Josh, please stop that vampire talk. You know it is just a story," Mr. Hudson said.

Josh shrugged. "I'm only trying to do my job."

# The Vampire Mystery

Mr. Hudson shook his head. "I don't think this kind of talk is helping."

Josh stood abruptly. "I'm sorry, but I have to get back to the office, now. Thanks for the lunch, Charles. Call me before you leave," he added. The screen door slammed behind him.

Mr. Hudson sighed. "Josh is so excitable," he said. "I should have hired a nice, calm Realtor to sell my house."

"Is there really a vampire around here?" Benny asked.

"Of course not," Grandfather answered. "Vampires are not real."

"Your grandfather is right," Mr. Hudson said. "When I was growing up in this house, there was an old legend about a vampire around here. People said he prowled the town at night and brought his victims to the cemetery. During the daytime, he hid in his coffin and slept. I always loved scary stories. As a matter of fact, I used to frighten my little brother by telling him all about the vampire. Sometimes, he was so afraid that he would have to sleep in my bed with me. I thought that the vampire story was so much fun that when I grew up I turned it into a book."

"*The Legend of the Vampire!*" Benny cried. "We checked it out of the library this morning. It's outside in my backpack."

"Yes, Benny. That's the one. It became a popular book. It has been so popular that I am hoping to convince a producer to turn my book into a movie."

"How exciting," said Jessie. "Would it be filmed here in Greenfield?"

Mr. Hudson refilled Benny's bowl with chowder. "I had hoped so," Mr. Hudson said. "I was supposed to go out of town to meet with some people to discuss the project. But with the house for sale, I'm not sure that I can leave just now. There's no one to look after the place while I'm away."

"We would be happy to do it," Henry offered.

"Yes," Jessie added. "We could check on it every day if you like."

"Are you sure?" Mr. Hudson asked. "You really wouldn't mind? I would be happy to pay you."

"We're sure," Violet said. "And you don't have to pay us anything. We can ride our bikes over. I'll water the flowers out front in the garden."

"And I can cut the lawn," Henry said.

"Benny and I will sweep the porch and dust the furniture for you," Jessie said.

Grandfather smiled. "My grandchildren are very helpful."

"I can see that," Mr. Hudson said. "And I'm very grateful. Now I can go away without worrying that I might lose a sale because the house is not in good shape."

After Grandfather left to attend a business meeting, Mr. Hudson walked with the Aldens to the back of the house. He opened the door to the shed. "The lawn mower is a little old," he said to Henry. "Sometimes it acts up."

"Don't worry, Mr. Hudson," Jessie said. "Henry is very good with motors and with fixing things."

The shed was large, but dark. Mr. Hudson called the children over to the corner. He lifted a clay flowerpot from a wooden shelf. "This is where I keep a spare key to the house," he said. "It will be right here under this pot whenever you need to get inside."

## An Offer to Help

"Wow, this is a cool bike," Violet said, running her hand over the shiny front fender of an old-fashioned blue bicycle.

"Yes," said Mr. Hudson. "It is very old, but I like to keep it in good shape. It belongs to my brother. It's odd, though. I thought that I had stored the bicycle in the back of the shed. I wonder how it got up here."

"Does your brother live nearby?" asked Benny.

Mr. Hudson dropped his hands into his pockets. He looked at the ground for a few moments before answering. "No. I'm sorry to say that my brother and I had a fight a long time ago when we were younger. My brother left town, and I never heard from him again. It was a silly fight. I don't even remember what it was about anymore. It happened over forty years ago."

Suddenly, everyone heard loud shouts coming from the front of the house. They ran from the shed. An older woman was pointing at the Aldens' bicycles and calling out for Mr. Hudson.

"Look at this!" she cried. "Bicycles are blocking the sidewalk! How am I supposed to get my

shopping cart past? I think I hurt my ankle on this one." Mrs. Fairfax pointed at Benny's small bike.

"Hold on, Martha," Mr. Hudson said. "We'll get them out of your way."

Henry, Jessie, Violet, and Benny quickly moved their bicycles onto the lawn. Mrs. Fairfax glared at them.

"We're so sorry," Jessie said. "It was careless of us to leave our bikes there. We hope your ankle doesn't hurt too badly."

"Children are always careless!" Mrs. Fairfax said. "These children aren't moving in here, are they, Charles?" she asked.

"These are the Aldens," Mr. Hudson said. "They are the grandchildren of James Alden, an old friend of mine. They will be looking after my house while I am away on business."

Mrs. Fairfax pushed her glasses up on her nose and stared at each of the Aldens. "Well, you better make sure they don't leave their things lying around in my way."

"We won't do that, Mrs. Fairfax," Henry promised.

Mrs. Fairfax marched up the sidewalk and into her home.

Mr. Hudson sighed. "I'm sorry about that, children," he said. "Mrs. Fairfax is not a bad lady. She was a good friend of my brothers and has lived next door to me for fifty years. But she is worried that I might sell my home to a noisy family with lots of children and barking dogs. She likes her peace and quiet."

"We'll park our bikes behind the house from now on," Henry said. "We should never have left them on the sidewalk."

The four Aldens said good-bye to Mr. Hudson. As they pedaled toward home, they saw Mrs. Fairfax staring at them from the front window of her house.

# CHAPTER 3

# A Missing Book

After dinner, the Aldens each took a slice of Mrs. McGregor's apple pie and headed outside to the front porch. Watch, their wirehaired terrier, raced outdoors with them.

"How did the smallest Alden end up with the biggest piece of pie?" asked Henry.

Benny, his cheeks stuffed with the delicious dessert, shrugged his shoulders.

"Henry," asked Violet, "what do you really think about the vampire story? It seems like Mr. Hudson did see something in the cemetery that scared him."

"I'm sure the vampire's not real, Violet. But something odd does seem to be going on at Mr. Hudson's house."

"Yes," said Jessie. "Why would someone steal the 'For Sale' sign on his front lawn?"

"I'm not sure," said Henry. "Maybe it was just a joke."

Violet shook her head. "Josh certainly wasn't laughing."

"No," Jessie replied. "And Josh seemed really upset by the vampire story. I wish we knew a little more about that legend. It might help us to solve the mystery of what is going on at Mr. Hudson's house."

Benny jumped from his chair and dashed into the house. He returned with his backpack. Watch barked excitedly.

"Benny, what are you doing?" asked Jessie.

"It's a clue!" Benny replied. "The book I got at the library yesterday that Mr. Hudson wrote. I put it in my backpack."

"That's right, Benny!" Henry said. "I had forgotten about *The Legend of the Vampire*."

"And didn't Mr. Hudson say that he based his book on the old vampire legend?" asked Violet.

"Yes, he did," said Jessie. "Good work, Benny."

Benny reached into his backpack. A funny look

came over his face.

"What's wrong?" asked Jessie.

"I know I put the book in my backpack," he said. "But now it's not here."

"Maybe you took it out when you got home," suggested Violet.

"No, I'm sure I didn't," Benny said.

"Could it have fallen out?" asked Jessie.

"I don't think so," Benny said. "There are no holes in my backpack. But maybe I didn't zip it closed all the way."

"We should ride our bikes back to the library and to Mr. Hudson's," Henry suggested. "We can look along the streets to check if the book fell out."

Henry, Jessie, Violet, and Benny strapped on their helmets and rode to the library. It was almost closing time.

"Hello, children," said Mrs. Skylar. "The library will be closing in about ten minutes. Can I help you find something?"

"No, thank you, Mrs. Skylar," said Henry. "We were wondering if anyone turned in *The Legend of the Vampire*."

Mrs. Skylar went to her computer and clicked the keys. "No," she said. "The computer shows that it was checked out this morning by Benny. Did something happen to the book?"

"We seem to have misplaced it," said Jessie. "But I'm sure we'll find it soon."

"I hope so," said Mrs. Skylar. "Good luck."

"Don't look so sad, Benny," said Jessie. "We still might find the book outside Mr. Hudson's house."

The four Aldens rode quickly through Greenfield until they arrived at Whittaker Street. It was still light out, but the sun was beginning to set behind Mr. Hudson's house.

The woods and the cemetery were full of shadows.

Henry, Jessie, Violet, and Benny spread out and searched the sidewalk and the lawn. There was no sign of the book.

"Maybe Mr. Hudson found it already," Violet suggested. "He might have the book inside."

Henry knocked on the door, but no one answered. It was very quiet.

Suddenly, a loud clatter came from the side yard.

The children ran to the edge of the porch. Their bicycles were lying in a heap on the ground.

"That's odd," said Henry.

"Maybe it was the wind," Violet suggested.

Benny jumped over the porch rail and picked up his bike. "It's not very windy." Something caught his eye, and he pointed toward the cemetery. "Look!"

"What do you see?" asked Jessie.

But whatever it was, it was gone.

"I don't know," Benny said. "I thought I saw someone in a dark cape running. But I guess it was just a shadow."

"We should get home," Henry said. "Grandfather doesn't like us riding our bikes in the dark. And it is getting late."

"But what about the book?" asked Benny. "We still haven't found it."

"Don't worry," said Jessie. "If we don't find it by the due date, we'll all chip in from our allowance money to pay for the book."

"Hey! Is that you Alden children over there making all that clatter?" Mrs. Fairfax was leaning against the rail of her front porch.

"We're sorry," Henry called. "The wind knocked our bicycles over. We're leaving now."

"I hope so," she said, turning away and stomping back toward her front door. "A person can't get any peace around here. And stop running through my backyard!"

"But we..." Violet wanted to explain that they had not run through her yard, but Mrs. Fairfax was already inside, the screen door slamming shut behind her.

"Why is she so angry?" asked Benny.

"Mrs. Fairfax probably just likes her peace and quiet," Violet said. "I suppose she's not used to such noises on this street. Maybe we frightened her."

"I hope I don't upset her when I have to cut the lawn," Henry added. "Lawn mowers make plenty of noise."

"So does my stomach," said Benny. "All this bike riding has made me hungry."

Henry laughed. "Let's go home and get you another piece of Mrs. McGregor's pie."

# CHAPTER 4

# Lost!

The next morning Mrs. McGregor placed a large platter of steaming waffles on the breakfast table.

"Here you go, Benny," she said. "I made a special waffle for you."

Benny had been sitting with his head in his hands. He looked up to see what Mrs. McGregor had made. It was a large round waffle with strawberries for eyes and a blueberry mouth. Fluffy white whipped cream hair sat on top.

"Wow! Thank you, Mrs. McGregor." Benny grabbed his fork.

"There's the smile we like to see," said Grandfather. "Are you feeling better now?"

Benny's mouth was stuffed full with waffle

and fruit.

Jessie answered for him. "Benny's not sick, Grandfather. He feels bad because he can't find *The Legend of the Vampire*, the book he checked out of the library yesterday."

"Perhaps it's in your room, Benny," Grandfather suggested.

Benny shook his head.

Violet spooned fruit over her waffle. "We searched everywhere," she said.

"It was in his backpack when we were at Mr. Hudson's house. By the time we got home, it had mysteriously disappeared. We even checked at the library to see if anyone had turned it in." Henry poured himself a glass of orange juice.

"That *is* a mystery," Grandfather said. "But I'm sure you children will figure it out."

The Aldens loved mysteries, and they had already solved quite a few since coming to live with Grandfather.

"Maybe you can check at the library again today," Grandfather said. "They are having their annual fair and bake sale on the front lawn. It might be fun to stop by."

A timer in the kitchen rang. "That must be my pie," Mrs. McGregor said, wiping her hands on her apron. "I made an apple pie and a lemon cake to donate to the bake sale. If you children want, you can come with me this morning when I drop them off at the library."

"That reminds me," Grandfather said. "Mr. Hudson called this morning. He will be leaving on his business trip shortly. He asked if you children could stop by the house later today to cut the lawn and make sure everything is neat and in order. A young couple from out of town will be stopping by to look at the house this afternoon. Mr. Hudson is hoping that they will be interested in buying it."

"Are you sure Mr. Hudson called this morning?" asked Henry. "We thought he might have left for his trip last night."

"No," Grandfather said. "It was this morning. He said he was packing his bags as he spoke to me."

"We'll go to Mr. Hudson's after the library," Henry said.

"It's such a beautiful house," Violet added. "We'll

make sure it is in good shape when that couple arrives. I'm sure they'll love it."

Henry, Jessie, Violet, and Benny helped Mrs. McGregor with the dishes and then carefully placed the baked goods in the car.

"The car smells so good!" Benny exclaimed as Mrs. McGregor drove into town.

Violet laughed. "You're right, Benny. It smells like a bakery in here."

Mrs. McGregor parked the car by the curb across the street from the library. Henry carried the apple pie, and Jessie took the lemon cake.

Balloons were everywhere. They were tied to the tables and the streetlamps and to the backs of chairs. Colorful streamers hung from the library windows and rippled in the wind. On one side of the lawn, a man with a beard played a guitar while children sang along. A storyteller in a long dress sat in a circle and used puppets to tell her tale.

"Hello!" Mrs. Skylar called. "I'm so glad you could come to the library fair."

"We wouldn't think of missing it," Mrs. McGregor said.

"Mrs. McGregor made this cake and the pie," Jessie explained. "They're for the bake sale table."

"They look beautiful!" Mrs. Skylar exclaimed. "I'm sure we'll get a very large donation for them."

Mrs. McGregor beamed.

"Do you think this is a big enough donation for Mrs. McGregor's lemon cake?" Benny pulled a fist from his pocket. He opened his hand to show three nickels, a dime, two quarters, a rubber band, a gum wrapper, and a small rock.

Mrs. McGregor laughed. "Oh, Benny," she said. "I can make another lemon cake for you at home."

Henry plucked the rock and the gum wrapper from Benny's hand. He chuckled. "I don't think these are worth very much, Benny," he said.

"The rock does have pretty colors in it, though." Violet smiled at her little brother.

"Why don't we take the pie and the cake over to the bake-sale table for Mrs. McGregor," Jessie suggested. "Maybe you can buy some cookies or a cupcake with your coins."

"Okay. Let's go!" Benny darted off through the crowd.

# Lost!

"Benny! Wait for us!" Henry called. But it was too late. Thinking only of cookies, Benny had run far ahead.

Henry, Jessie, and Violet said good-bye to Mrs. McGregor and thanked her for the ride to the library fair. Then they headed toward the bake sale. They set Mrs. McGregor's pie and cake on the table.

"Where's Benny?" asked Jessie.

"I don't know," Henry replied. "I thought for sure we would see him here picking out some cookies."

"Excuse me," Violet said to the lady behind the table. "Was there a six-year-old boy with dark-brown hair here a few moments ago?"

"The table has been crowded," the lady said. "I'm not sure. Is that him over there?" She pointed through the crowd.

Violet ran toward the little boy, but it was not Benny.

Henry and Jessie looked worried.

"Maybe he couldn't find the bake-sale table," Violet said. "He's probably wandering nearby."

"Let's split up," Henry said. "We'll each go a

different way and meet back here in ten minutes."

"Benny! Benny!" Henry, Jessie, and Violet ran through the crowd calling their brother's name. But he was nowhere in sight.

# A Vial of Blood?

Jessie found Benny walking down the sidewalk. There was a scrape on his knee and a trickle of blood running down his leg.

"Benny!" she cried. "Where have you been? We were so worried. What happened to your leg?"

Just then, Henry and Violet came running up to them.

Jessie settled Benny on a soft patch of grass under a tree. Violet ran to borrow the first-aid kit from Mrs. Skylar.

"Are you okay?" Henry asked.

Benny nodded bravely. He was almost as breathless as Violet when she returned with the first aid kit.

Jessie cleaned the blood from his knee and squirted a bit of antiseptic on his cut. She covered it up with a bandage.

"I was running to the bake-sale table," Benny said. "I guess I wasn't watching where I was going. I crashed smack into a man and fell to the ground."

"Is that how you hurt your knee?" Violet asked.

Benny nodded. "The man leaned down to help me up. I was so surprised. It was Mr. Hudson!"

"Mr. Hudson?" Henry said. "But he's away on his business trip. Are you sure it was him?"

Benny scratched his head. "Now I'm not so sure. I thought so at first. I called him Mr. Hudson when I apologized. When I said that name, he looked upset. He turned and left really fast."

"But where have you been?" asked Jessie. "We looked all over for you."

"I followed him," Benny said.

"Benny! You shouldn't have done that. You should have stayed here by the library," Jessie said.

"I know. I'm sorry, Jessie. But the man dropped something. I tried to catch up with him so I could give it back. I didn't go far."

# A Vial of Blood?

"Did you catch him?" asked Violet.

"No. He had an old blue bike down the street behind a tree. He rode away."

"What did he drop?" asked Henry.

Benny held out his hand. "This," he said. Henry took the small plastic bottle from his brother. It was filled with a red liquid.

"What do you think it could be?" Jessie asked.

"I don't know," said Henry.

"I do," said Violet, putting her hand to her mouth. "It looks like...like...blood!"

The Alden children stared at each other for a few seconds. "I know it looks like blood," Henry said. "But it is probably something else. It could be ink."

"Or medicine," Jessie added. "Remember your cough syrup from last winter, Violet? It was red."

"I suppose that's true," Violet said. "But that is an odd bottle for cough medicine."

Henry put the bottle in his pocket. "I'll hold on to it in case we see the man again."

"Let's go to the diner," Jessie said. "I think we could all use a cool drink and some time to think."

"And some food!" Benny added.

# A Vial of Blood?

It was lunchtime, and the diner was very crowded. Nancy, a thin waitress with short blond hair, showed the Aldens to a booth in the back.

"How's this kids?" she asked.

"It's perfect. Thank you," said Jessie.

After they had placed their order, Jessie pulled out her notebook and a pencil. When facing a mystery, the Aldens often found that writing all the facts and clues on paper helped them to see what was going on.

Jessie wrote "Vampire Legend" at the top of the page. "What do we know about the vampire legend?" she asked.

Henry took a long drink of his lemonade. "People around Greenfield used to tell stories about a vampire. We know that vampires are not real, so the people must have done it for fun or to scare each other."

"And Mr. Hudson heard those stories when he was growing up. He turned them into a book," Violet added.

"Then Mr. Hudson saw a vampire in the cemetery behind his house." Benny leaned across the table, his eyes wide.

"No, Benny. He saw something that concerned him. He didn't actually see a vampire," Henry said.

"Then what did he see?" asked Benny.

"We're not sure," Henry said.

Nancy stopped at the table with an armful of plates. "Here you go, kids," she said, setting down the plates of burgers and sandwiches.

Violet chewed thoughtfully on her grilled cheese. "One thing we do know," she said. "Mr. Hudson is trying to sell his house, but strange things are happening there that keep buyers away."

Jessie made a list. "There was the 'vampire' in the cemetery," she said. "And the broken flowerpots on the front porch."

"And someone keeps stealing the 'For Sale' sign." Violet finished her sandwich and placed her napkin on her plate.

"But why would anyone care if Mr. Hudson sold his house?" asked Benny.

"Mrs. Fairfax does not want him to move," Jessie said.

"That's true," Henry replied. "Do you think she could be the one behind all the strange happenings?"

# A Vial of Blood?

Benny suddenly sat up very straight. "It's him," he whispered. "The man from the library."

"Where?" asked Henry who was across the table from Benny and facing the opposite direction.

"He's at the other end of the diner, sitting at the counter. I could give him back his bottle of blood...I mean, red stuff." Benny slid out of the booth. "Hurry, Henry. Give it to me. He's just about to leave."

Henry reached into his pocket, but it was too late. The man quickly jumped off his stool, his head lowered into his shirt, and darted out of the diner.

A few minutes later, Nancy stopped at the table to clear the plates. "Would you like to order dessert?" she asked.

"No, thank you," Jessie answered. "Not today."

"Excuse me," Henry asked. "Did you happen to wait on the man who was at the end of the counter? The one who left a few minutes ago?"

Nancy looked toward the empty stool. "Yes, I did," she answered. "Why do you want to know?"

"We have something of his," Henry said. "He

dropped it earlier today, and we wanted to give it back. Do you know where we can find him?"

"No," Nancy replied. "I'm sorry. I never saw him before. But it's odd that you say that. I have something for him too. He left the diner so quickly that he forgot to take his book with him."

"His book?" asked Violet.

"Yes." Nancy reached into the deep pocket of her apron. "It's a library book. He left it on the counter beside his plate."

She set the book on the table.

Jessie gasped. "*The Legend of the Vampire!*"

Benny pulled the book toward him and stared down at the bloodred fangs of the man on the cover. "We could take it back to the library for you," he offered.

"Why, thanks," said Nancy. "I appreciate that. It will save me a trip. If the man comes back, I'll tell him that his book is at the library. Have a good day, kids."

When Nancy had left, Benny leaned across the table. "It's not *his* book. It's mine!"

# CHAPTER 6

# Accused

The Aldens walked slowly to Mr. Hudson's house on Whittaker Street.

"I don't understand why he would take Benny's book," Jessie said.

"Maybe it was an accident," Violet offered. "Maybe the book dropped out of Benny's bag and the man found it."

The children had no more time to talk. As they turned the corner onto Whittaker Street, they saw police cars in front of Mr. Hudson's house!

"There they are! They're the ones who did it!" Mrs. Fairfax stood on the sidewalk pointing at the Aldens.

The police turned to look at the children. A

tall officer with black hair held a pad and a pen. "Excuse me, but who are you?" he asked.

"We're the Aldens," Henry said. He introduced himself and his sisters and brother. "Is something wrong, Officer?"

Officer Franklin wrote their names on his pad. Then he looked up. "Someone vandalized this house last night."

"Oh, my!" Violet cried. A number of Mr. Hudson's beautiful flowers had been ripped from the ground and were lying across the walkway.

Benny was the first to see the words written across the porch boards in bright red letters. "'Leave...me...to...rest...in...pea...pea...'" He turned to Henry for help.

"'Leave me to rest in peace,'" Henry read. "'Or you will be sorry.'"

"It was those children who did it!" Mrs. Fairfax said. "I saw them here last night. They were right there on the porch."

Officer Franklin looked at Henry. "Were you here last night?" he asked.

"Yes, Officer," Henry replied. "But we sure didn't

do this."

"Then what were you doing here?" the officer asked.

Just then the front door of Mr. Hudson's house opened. Josh rushed out.

"Thank goodness you children are here!" he said.

"You know them?" Officer Franklin asked Josh.

"Of course!" Josh replied. "These are the Aldens. Mr. Hudson told me that they would be stopping by today."

"And you don't suspect that they could have caused this damage?" the officer asked.

"What? No! Of course not. Mr. Hudson trusts them and so do I. He asked them to look after his place while he was away."

"Sorry, children," Officer Franklin said. "I hope you understand that it is my job to ask questions."

"We understand," Henry said.

Mrs. Fairfax banged her cane against the ground. "Seems to me you don't ask enough questions!" she said. "This used to be a nice, quiet street until that Realtor and those children started coming around.

They're up to something. You need to investigate them!" She stomped back to her house.

Josh ran his hands through his hair. "What am I going to do?" he asked. "The Bensons will be here in a few hours to look at the house. When they see this, they will never want to buy it."

"We'll clean it up," Jessie said. "We'll start right away."

"No," Josh said. "We can't clean it up. It is evidence. The police might need it. We should leave everything just the way it is."

Officer Franklin overheard them. "It's okay for you children to clean up the mess," he said. "We have taken pictures of everything. That is all we need."

Josh bit down on his lower lip and kicked at one of the upturned plants. "Are you sure?" he asked. "We want you to find the person who did this."

"I'm sure," Officer Franklin replied. "We have all the information that we need."

The police officers left, and Josh dropped onto the porch steps. "This is too much," he said.

"What do you mean?" asked Henry.

# The Vampire Mystery

"Don't you see?" Josh asked. "It's the vampire!"

"But there's no such thing," Jessie said.

Josh's face was white. "It's right from the book," he said. "I've read it."

"*The Legend of the Vampire*?" asked Benny.

"Yes," Josh answered. "In the book, a vampire has his coffin hidden in the basement of an old home. A lonely old man lives by himself in the house. There is a cemetery behind the house. The vampire only comes out at night when the old man is sleeping. But one day the old man decides to sell the house. The vampire does not want his peace disturbed. He bites the neck of anyone who comes to live in the house."

Violet shivered. "What a terrible story!"

"What happens in the end?" Benny asked.

"No one will live in the house," Josh said. "The vampire has it all to himself." Josh looked over his shoulder and lowered his voice. "And the vampire still roams the cemetery every night!"

Jessie put her arm around Benny. "But it's just a story!" she said. "Everyone knows that vampires are not real."

Josh looked down. "I guess you're right, Jessie," he said. He grabbed an uprooted plant that was sitting on the step and tossed it angrily onto the lawn.

Violet picked it up.

"We should get to work," Henry said. "I need to cut the lawn."

"I'll replace the flowers the best that I can," Violet promised.

Jessie stared at the red letters on the porch. "I'll take care of cleaning that."

"What about me?" asked Benny.

Henry put his hand on Benny's shoulder. "Come with me, Benny," he said. "You can rake up the grass as I cut it."

"And I've got to make some phone calls." Josh stood and pulled a cell phone from his pocket. He pointed to the front lawn. "Can you believe that someone stole the 'For Sale' sign again? I'm running out of signs. I'm not sure that I even have any left."

The Aldens walked around to the shed to find the tools they needed. After the bright sunshine, the shed seemed very dark.

"Ouch!" Henry cried.

"Are you okay?" asked Jessie.

"Yes...I just stubbed my toe on the bike," Henry said.

"I don't remember the bike being in that spot yesterday," Violet said.

Henry wheeled the bike to the corner. "You're right, Violet. I think it was on the other side of the shed yesterday. That's odd."

Violet felt something fall down her neck. She cried out.

"What is it, Violet?" asked Jessie. "Are you okay?"

Violet laughed. "Yes," she said. "I guess I'm a little jumpy. It's the chain for the lightbulb. I must have backed into it. It tickled the back of my neck." Violet pulled the chain several times. It clicked, but nothing happened.

"The bulb must be out," said Henry.

"It's okay," Violet replied. "I've found the trowel and some gardening gloves. That's all I need. I'm going to go put those plants back in the ground right away. I don't want the roots to dry out and die. I know how proud Mr. Hudson is of his flowers."

There was a crash against the side of the shed. "I've found the rake!" Benny cried. "I'm all ready to help you, Henry."

Violet carried her tools to the front yard. She decided to work on the plants closest to the porch first. She knelt down and began to dig. She could hear Josh talking on his cell phone inside the house. His voice got louder as he came closer to the screen door on the porch.

"Yes," Josh said. "Mr. Hudson will have to lower the price now. Who will want to buy a house that has a vampire in the backyard?"

Then he laughed. "No," he said. "I don't really believe in vampires. But this is working out very well for us. When Mr. Hudson comes back from his trip, I will convince him that he should offer his house for much less money. Then you can buy it."

Violet stood up. What was Josh talking about?

"Violet!" Josh said. He quickly flipped his cell phone closed. "I didn't see you there!" He walked out onto the porch.

"I'm sorry," Violet said. "I didn't mean to startle you. I was replanting the flowers."

Josh stuck his hands deep into his pockets. He looked around the corner of the house. "Are the others still out back?" he asked.

"Yes," Violet said.

"You shouldn't sneak around like that," Josh said. "Especially not with all the things that are going on around here."

"I wasn't sneaking," Violet tried to explain, but Josh's cell phone buzzed.

He looked at the number on the screen, but he did not answer it. He rubbed his stomach instead. "I am so hungry," he said. "I think I will walk over to the diner for a sandwich."

Henry pushed the lawn mower to the front yard. Benny pulled the rake behind him.

"This is going to be fun!" Benny said. "I wish there was a yard full of leaves for me to rake. Then I could make a big pile and jump in it."

"You'll have to wait a few weeks for the leaves to fall," Henry said.

"I'm going to ask Mr. Hudson if I can come back then and rake for him," Benny said.

Henry smiled. "I'm sure he would like that. But

maybe he will have sold his house by then."

Violet was about to tell Henry about the person Josh had been speaking to on his cell phone. But just then Henry pulled the cord on the lawn mower. It roared to life.

"Sorry for the noise, Violet!" Henry shouted. "I will try to stay away from the flowers!"

Jessie had gone into the house and found a bucket and a scrub brush. A bottle of cleaner was under the kitchen sink. She filled the bucket with hot soapy water. Then she set to work trying to clean the red words from the porch.

Violet carefully placed the flowers back into the garden. Some of their stems were broken. It made her sad. She smoothed the loose dirt around each plant. Then she found a watering can in the shed and gave each plant a drink. She worked so hard that she forgot all about the conversation that she had overheard.

Mrs. Fairfax came out on her front porch every once in a while. She watched the Aldens with a wary look on her face. But the children were careful not to make too much noise and to stay off

# The Vampire Mystery

Mrs. Fairfax's property.

"There," Henry said, brushing loose grass from his jeans. "I think the house looks fine now."

"I don't know, Henry." Jessie shook her head. "The lawn looks nice and the flowers are beautiful. But I could not wash the letters off completely. If you look closely, you can still read what it says."

Henry walked up the steps to the porch. "I see what you mean. The porch might need to be repainted."

"We could never do that in time. The buyers will be here soon." Jessie sighed.

"I know what we can do!" Benny flung the door open and ran into the house. He returned a minute later. "How about this?" he asked. He held up a small rug.

"Great thinking, Benny!" Henry said.

"I remembered that it was in the kitchen by the sink," Benny said. "It will look nice out here too."

Jessie took the rug and spread it in front of the porch door. "It doesn't cover everything," she said. "But it is a big improvement. Way to go, Benny."

Jessie locked the door and put the key back under the pot in the shed. Henry tied the bag of grass clippings and walked it to the curb.

"Isn't this Josh's car?" Henry asked.

"Yes," Violet answered. "Josh hasn't left yet. He walked to the diner for a sandwich about a half an hour ago."

"What's that in the back seat?" asked Benny.

The windows were up, but the Aldens could see something large in the back of Josh's car. Most of it was covered with a blanket. But two black metal stakes poked out from beneath the covering.

"It looks like a 'For Sale' sign is under that blanket," Jessie said.

The Aldens were puzzled.

"I thought Josh said he didn't have any more signs left," said Henry.

"It could be for a different house," Violet said. "I'm sure Josh has more than one house to sell. Or maybe it is a 'For Rent' sign for an apartment."

"You could be right, Violet," said Jessie.

Just then Josh came hurrying up the street. "What are you kids doing?" he called crossly. Josh quickly stood in front of his car with his hands on his hips.

"We're only putting the trash bag to the curb," Benny said. "Look at the lawn. Don't you think it looks good? I raked it!"

Josh's face relaxed. "Yes, Benny," he said. "Everything looks very nice again. Thank you. The Bensons should be here soon."

Jessie decided not to tell Josh about the red letters that did not wash off the porch. He still seemed too upset. He leaned back against his car and crossed his arms. His foot tapped nervously against the curb. And maybe Josh and the Bensons would not notice the few faint words that were not covered up by the rug.

The Aldens said good-bye to Josh and headed home.

# Three Suspects

Grandfather arrived for dinner just as Mrs. McGregor was setting a pot roast on the table.

"Smells great!" Grandfather said. "I'm sorry I'm late. My meeting lasted longer than I had thought."

Just then, there was a loud clap of thunder, and the lights flickered off and on for a minute. Rain drummed against the side of the house. The children quickly closed all the windows.

"You got home just in time, Grandfather." Violet spread her napkin on her lap. "One moment later and you would have been caught in the storm."

"That's true. My timing was perfect." Grandfather smiled. "I'm glad my grandchildren are not out in this storm."

During dinner, the children told Grandfather about the vandalism at Mr. Hudson's home and the work that they had done to clean it up.

"That was very kind of you," Grandfather said. "I wonder who would do such a thing?"

"We've been wondering the same thing, Grandfather," said Henry.

Jessie spooned some warm applesauce onto Benny's plate. "We think that whoever it is does not want Mr. Hudson to sell his house."

Violet was thinking hard. She'd heard Josh on the phone the day before. She knew he had said something about selling the house. But she couldn't remember what he'd said.

Grandfather shook his head. "I suppose the vandalism is why Mr. Hudson cut short his business trip."

"Mr. Hudson is home?" asked Henry.

"I thought so." Grandfather passed the mashed potatoes to Benny. "But I could be wrong. Driving home this evening, I thought I saw Mr. Hudson walking down the street near the library. I called out to him, but he turned a corner and disappeared."

## Three Suspects

After dinner, Grandfather went into his study to make some phone calls. Mrs. McGregor brought out an iced lemon cake and four plates.

"You brought home the lemon cake from the bake sale?" Benny clapped his hands.

"No, Benny," Mrs. McGregor replied. "Someone bought that cake and donated twenty dollars to the library for it."

"Twenty dollars! That must have been the biggest donation at the bake sale!" Violet smiled at Mrs. McGregor.

Mrs. McGregor's face flushed red with pride. "I don't know about that," she said.

"I don't think twenty dollars is enough." Benny held out his empty plate. "I would pay one hundred dollars for your lemon cake!"

"That's why I made another one for you when I came home." Mrs. McGregor laughed. "And I'll even waive the hundred-dollar fee!"

The Aldens each ate a big slice of the good cake.

"Do you think the man that Grandfather saw today was Mr. Hudson?" asked Violet.

"I don't know," Henry said. "If it was Mr. Hudson,

why didn't he say hello when Grandfather called out to him?"

"Maybe he didn't hear Grandfather," said Jessie.

"I thought I saw Mr. Hudson too," said Benny. "But now I know it wasn't him."

"How do you know?" Jessie refilled Benny's glass with milk.

"The man I saw did not dress like Mr. Hudson. His clothes were old and not very clean. There was dirt on them and even some stains that looked like oil."

Violet tapped her fork on the table, thinking. "You're probably right, Benny. Mr. Hudson seems to be a very neat person. I don't think he would wear dirty clothes."

Benny took a big gulp of milk. "He did look like Mr. Hudson, but it was probably just his white hair and mustache that confused me."

"I wonder if the Bensons showed up to look at the house this afternoon," Jessie said.

Benny wiped away his milk mustache. "I hope that Josh didn't say anything about vampires to them."

## Three Suspects

"Josh wouldn't do that," Henry said. "Not if he wants to sell the house for Mr. Hudson. Doesn't he want everyone to be interested in buying it?"

This reminded Violet of something. Something important. Suddenly she remembered what Josh had said on the phone. "Maybe he doesn't!" Violet said.

Henry, Jessie, and Benny looked very surprised.

"Why not, Violet?" asked Jessie. "Selling the house is Josh's job."

At last Violet told the others about the conversation she had overheard. "He told the person on the phone that everything was working out well. When Mr. Hudson came back from his trip, Josh would convince him to lower the price for the house."

"That is very suspicious," Henry admitted.

Jessie crossed her arms. "And Josh did act strange when he noticed us standing next to his car."

"He knows all about the legend of the vampire," Benny added. "Remember how he told us the whole story?"

"Maybe Josh is behind the vandalism," Henry

said. "He could be using scenes from the book to scare people away. If no one wants to buy the house, Mr. Hudson will have to offer it for a very low price."

Violet nodded. "And the person who Josh was speaking to on the phone would get a great house for not much money. That would be so unfair!"

"Maybe if we read Mr. Hudson's book, we can find more clues to this mystery," Henry said. "We might be able to find out what Josh will be up to next."

"If it *is* Josh, that is," Jessie added. "But what if it's Mrs. Fairfax? She doesn't want the house sold either. And since she lives next door, it would be easy for her to cause the damage and sneak back home."

"That's true." Violet folded her napkin. "And Mrs. Fairfax always hears us when we are at Mr. Hudson's house. Don't you think she would have heard the person who broke the flowerpots and wrote on the porch?"

"There is another suspect as well," Henry said. "We shouldn't forget about the man who ran into Benny at the library fair."

"But what could he have to do with it?" asked Benny.

## Three Suspects

Henry looked thoughtful. "I don't really know. But it is suspicious that he ran away from you when you called him by Mr. Hudson's name. And don't forget that he had your library book. He must have taken it from your backpack at Mr. Hudson's while we were inside having lunch."

"The book! It's gone again! I can't believe it!" Benny slapped the side of his head.

"What's wrong?" asked Jessie.

"I left it on the kitchen table at Mr. Hudson's house. I set it down there so I could pull up the rug to use to cover the words written on the front porch. Afterward, I forgot to go back inside for the book."

Henry laughed. "I think there is something mysterious about that book. It never stays in the same place."

"Can we go get it?" asked Benny.

"I suppose we can," said Henry. "But it will be dark soon. We can't ride our bikes."

Violet looked out the window. "The rain seems to have stopped."

The children cleaned up their dessert plates and

put the cake away. They each found a flashlight to take on their nighttime walk. The air was slightly cool, and the storm clouds were moving away. A round, full moon shone over Greenfield.

**CHAPTER**

# Intruder

"What's that?" Violet asked as the children walked up Whittaker Street. "Did you see that light in Mr. Hudson's house?

The others had not seen it. "Maybe it was the moon shining on the window glass," Jessie suggested.

Violet was not so sure. But now the light was gone.

The rain had made the ground wet and muddy. The children's shoes squished in the lawn as they made their way toward the shed to retrieve the key to the house.

They each flicked on their flashlights. Jessie shone her beam on the shed door. Henry lifted

185

the latch, and the door squeaked open. The four Aldens stepped into the dark shed.

"Careful," Jessie warned. "Don't trip over the bicycle again."

"That's odd." Henry pointed his flashlight at the bike. "Didn't we move the bike to the left side of the shed today?"

"We did," Jessie agreed.

"Well, now it is on the right side of the shed."

Benny stood beside the bike. "And it's wet!" He shone his flashlight on the roof above the bike. "Even though there aren't any leaks in the roof."

"Someone has been riding this bike." Henry ran his hand over the dripping handlebars.

Violet walked over to look at the bike, but stumbled over an old suitcase. "What is this doing in the middle of the floor?"

"A suitcase?" Benny grabbed the handle and moved the suitcase against the wall. It was heavy. "Wouldn't Mr. Hudson have taken his suitcase with him when he went on his trip?"

"It looks old," Henry said. "Maybe Mr. Hudson has a newer one that he uses."

# The Vampire Mystery

Jessie shone her light on the flowerpot. She lifted it up. "It's gone!" she cried. "The key is not here. I know I put it right back under this pot before we left this afternoon."

"Are you sure?" Henry felt around on a lower shelf. "Maybe it fell down here."

Violet and Benny searched the floor.

"I'm positive," Jessie said. "Someone has taken it!"

The Aldens hurried from the shed. They quickly shut and latched the door and ran to the front of the house.

"Look at this!" Benny did not even need his flashlight. In the light of the moon, the children could clearly see a set of muddy footprints leading right up to Mr. Hudson's front door!

Henry put his hand carefully on the doorknob and turned. It was not locked. He entered the house. "Hello! Mr. Hudson! Are you home?" Henry turned to the others. "There's no one here."

"Let's get Benny's book and get home," Violet said.

Jessie flipped the light switch, but nothing happened. "The lights are out!"

"It's probably the circuit breaker," Henry said. "Sometimes a storm can shut it off, especially in an old house like this. I know where the switch is. Mr. Hudson pointed it out when he was showing me around the house. I might be able to get the lights back on."

Henry and Jessie carefully walked down the stairs into the basement. Violet and Benny waited by the front door.

"Did you hear that?" Violet asked, looking over her shoulder.

Benny cocked his head. "Yes. It sounds like footsteps. Do you think it could be Henry and Jessie?"

"No," Violet whispered. "I think it is coming from outside. I wish Henry and Jessie would hurry up."

"You don't think it could be the vampire, do you?" asked Benny.

"There's no such thing," Violet said, but her voice was shaking. She turned and shut the front door, quickly turning the bolt.

A shaft of moonlight was shining through the window, and it fell across the carpeted floor. The rest of the house was dark. As Violet and Benny watched, a dark shadow flitted slowly across the moonlit carpet.

"What was that?" asked Benny, grabbing Violet's hand.

"I'm not sure," Violet answered. "Maybe it was a cloud passing in front of the moon."

"But it was shaped like a bat!" Benny cried.

Violet didn't want to frighten Benny, but she knew he was right. A large bat had just slowly passed by the window.

Suddenly the lights flashed on. Henry and Jessie pounded up the basement stairs.

"It was only the switch, just as I thought," Henry said, coming through the door. He stopped in his tracks when he saw the kitchen. Sitting on the table was a glass of milk and a plate with a half-eaten sandwich. Next to them was Benny's library book, *The Legend of the Vampire*, open to page 136.

Violet gasped. "Someone was here!"

"You're right, Violet." Henry walked to the table. "And whoever it was left in a hurry. This glass of milk is still cold."

## Intruder

"And here is the missing key!" Jessie picked up the key from the kitchen counter.

"I think we should go," Violet said.

Henry agreed. "We need to let Mr. Hudson know that someone has been inside his house."

"And it wasn't a vampire," Benny said, nodding at Violet, "because vampires don't eat sandwiches." He picked up his library book and stared at the front cover. "They only like blood!"

"Benny and I heard footsteps outside while you were in the basement," Violet explained. "We need to be very careful."

The children stepped outside and peered up and down the street. Jessie locked the door tightly and put the key into her pocket. She left the porch light on. The children hurried home as fast as they could.

# CHAPTER 9

# A Mysterious Photo

Later that night the Aldens sat in the living room each with a mug of hot chocolate and a plate of cookies. Henry opened *The Legend of the Vampire* to Chapter One. He began to read.

The cemetery on Whittaker Street was dark and cold. Martha stood by the gate and pulled her coat close around her body. She wrapped her scarf tightly around her neck. A chill ran down her spine, and she turned just in time to see a strange man in a long, dark cape gliding toward her neighbor's quaint little house. At first she had hoped that it was Francis, coming home after all these years. But when she saw the pale, white skin, the bloodred lips, and the piercing black eyes of the stranger, she knew that it was not Francis. Those eyes held her for a moment, and as they did, Martha felt the blood pounding through her veins. Was it fear or excitement that made her heart flutter so violently? Just as suddenly as he arrived, the stranger disappeared into her neighbor's basement, so quickly that it seemed he simply melted himself through the walls.

"Oh my!" cried Mrs. McGregor standing in the doorway. "What a frightening book to be reading before bed. It would give me nightmares!"

Benny rubbed his eyes and yawned. "We're looking for clues to a mystery in the story. Strange things are happening at Mr. Hudson's house."

"I've heard about it," Mrs. McGregor said. "Oh yes, and a man named Josh called a few

minutes ago. He said Mr. Hudson is coming home tomorrow. It seems he didn't need to stay as long as he'd planned. Also, Josh said you left milk on the table and mud on the porch."

The children looked at each other.

"We'll go over there first thing in the morning." Jessie said.

Henry nodded. "We need to tell Mr. Hudson someone was in his house."

Mrs. McGregor held a bag of mini marshmallows in her hand. "Also, I thought you might like to have some of these in your hot chocolates. Good night, children."

They all thanked Mrs. McGregor and wished her a good night.

Jessie reached for the marshmallows and sprinkled a few on the top of her hot chocolate. "Josh must have been at Mr. Hudson's house tonight."

"But why would he go over there so late?" wondered Violet.

Henry shrugged. "It does seem odd. I doubt he'd show the house to a buyer late at night."

Benny dropped a few marshmallows into his mug and a whole handful into his mouth. "Maybe he was looking for the vampire."

Henry stood to take a cookie from the platter and *The Legend of the Vampire* fell to the floor. When he picked it up, he saw something sticking out from the pages. It was an old black-and-white photograph. The edges were a little crumpled, and a crease ran down one side.

"Look at this!"

Jessie, Violet, and Benny crowded around the photo in Henry's hand.

"That's Mr. Hudson's house!" Violet pointed to the home that was in the background of the photo.

"Who do you think those two boys are?" asked Benny.

Two young children were posed in front of the porch. One looked to be about Henry's age, fourteen, and the other one seemed to be a little younger than Benny. The younger boy had his hand resting on the seat of a shiny, new bicycle.

Violet gasped. She pointed to the older boy. "That must be Mr. Hudson."

# A Mysterious Photo

"I'm sure you're right!" Jessie exclaimed. "And the other one must be his little brother."

Benny's fingers were sticky from the marshmallows, so he did not touch the photo. But he pointed at the two boys. "They sure do look an awful lot alike."

"Yes," Violet agreed. "If they were the same age, I would think they were twins."

"But how did the picture get in the book?" Benny wondered. "Do you think it was stuck in that book in the library for all those years?"

Henry turned the photo over in his hand. "No. I don't think it was in the book before today. See this crease mark? I think the photo was folded and carried in someone's wallet for a long time."

Henry pulled his wallet from his back pocket. He slid the picture in and out of the billfold. "See? When it is folded at the crease, this photo fits perfectly in a wallet. You wouldn't need to fold it if you were going to keep it in a book."

"That makes a lot of sense, Henry," Violet said.

"Look, there's some faded writing on the bottom." Jessie took the picture and held it up to the light. "It's hard to read."

Benny ran from the room and quickly returned with a magnifying glass that he had gotten as a gift on his last birthday. "This will help!" he cried.

"Thanks, Benny." Henry held the magnifying glass over the faded writing. It helped the children see the faded ink. Slowly, the Aldens puzzled out each letter.

"*Charles*!" Jessie exclaimed. "The first word is *Charles*!"

"Mr. Hudson's first name is Charles," Violet remembered.

"*A...n...d*," Benny read. "*And*! I know that word."

Violet smiled. "Good job, Benny."

The last word was the most faded. Before long, though, the Aldens had spelled *F-r-a-n-c-i-s*.

"Francis must be Mr. Hudson's younger brother," Jessie said.

Henry was paging through *The Legend of the Vampire*, checking to see if any more pictures could be stuck between its pages. He did not find any. He paused at the dedication page. "Look at this."

Jessie read aloud: "'This book is dedicated to my

dear brother, Francis.'"

"We didn't even have to read the book to find clues in it!" Benny exclaimed.

Henry set the book back on the table with the picture carefully placed inside. "We'll have a lot to tell Mr. Hudson when we see him tomorrow morning."

# CHAPTER 10

# Caught!

The next morning, after a quick breakfast of cereal and fruit, the Aldens jumped on their bikes and quickly rode to Mr. Hudson's house. But there was a police car in front! It was just driving away as the children walked up the front steps.

Jessie knocked on the front door.

"Come on in, kids," Mr. Hudson called from the living room. He was sitting on the couch, his suitcase dumped on the floor beside the coffee table. His hair was uncombed, and there were dark circles under his eyes.

Josh stood in the corner with his hands thrust deeply into his pockets.

"Is everything all right?" Jessie asked. "We just

saw the police car."

"The police were here looking for fingerprints," Mr. Hudson said. "Someone has broken into my home!"

Josh stepped forward. "No locks or windows were broken," he said. He stared at the Aldens. "Someone must have left the door unlocked. And it wasn't me!"

Mr. Hudson looked at the children. "I don't blame you," he said. "I even forget to lock the door sometimes. I know you meant well."

"But we *did* lock the door!" Jessie insisted. "We are very responsible. The person who broke into your home knew where the key was hidden. He took it from the shed and let himself in. We found the key last night on the kitchen counter."

Mr. Hudson looked up sharply.

"You must have told some of your friends where that key was," Josh said accusingly. "Who else could know where the key was hidden?"

"I can promise you that we did not tell anyone," Jessie answered.

Mr. Hudson ran his hands through his hair.

"Someone was in the shed," he said. "My plane came in very early this morning. When I got home, I heard noises coming from the shed. I called the police right away. The person in the shed ran away through the cemetery when the police arrived. The officers chased him. I don't know if they caught him yet or not. Perhaps he found the key by accident and let himself in when I was away."

The Aldens looked at each other.

"Was the person who ran from the shed as tall as the vampire that you have been seeing in the cemetery lately?" asked Henry.

"What?" Mr. Hudson sat up very straight. "The vampire? Josh, have you been telling stories?"

"It's not just a story," Josh answered. "You told me yourself that you saw something strange in the cemetery at night."

"I saw a person," Mr. Hudson explained to the children. "He dressed and acted like the vampire from my book, *The Legend of the Vampire*. Whenever I tried to call out to him or to catch him, he ran away."

# Caught!

"Do you think the person in the shed could have been the one who acted like the vampire?" Henry asked.

"I suppose so," Mr. Hudson answered. "He was about the same height. But who would want to do such a thing? I don't understand."

Jessie put her hand on Mr. Hudson's shoulder. "Mr. Hudson, was there anyone at all besides you who knew where you hid the spare key?"

Mr. Hudson was quiet for some time. "Besides you four children, there might be one other person," he said. "But it couldn't have been him."

The Aldens weren't so sure. "Mr. Hudson," Henry said. "We think it may have been your brother Francis who took the spare key and let himself into your home."

"Francis? What? How do you know that name?" Mr. Hudson's eyes were wide with surprise.

Benny took the folded photo from the pages of the book and handed it to Mr. Hudson.

Mr. Hudson drew in his breath sharply. He cradled the photo gently in his hands. "Where did you get this?" he finally asked.

# Caught!

"We found it," Benny replied, "stuck between the pages of *The Legend of the Vampire*."

"This is a picture of my brother and me!" Mr. Hudson cried.

Just then there were heavy footsteps on the front porch. Two police officers opened the screen door and brought in a man in handcuffs. He was dirty and disheveled. He looked almost exactly like Mr. Hudson.

Mr. Hudson jumped to his feet. "Francis!" he cried. He threw his arms around his brother.

The officers looked confused.

"Please, officer," Mr. Hudson asked. "Take those handcuffs off. This has all been a big misunderstanding. This is my brother."

"You're not going to press charges?" asked the officer. "He has already admitted that he broke into your home."

"No, no, of course I'm not going to prosecute," Mr. Hudson said hurriedly. "There has been no crime here. My brother is welcome in this house at any time."

The officer shook his head disapprovingly, but

he removed the cuffs. Mr. Hudson thanked the police for all their help and showed them to the door.

After Francis was comfortably seated in a chair with a glass of lemonade and a clean shirt borrowed from his brother, the Aldens explained what they knew.

"While you were away," Henry said, "Benny ran into a man at the library fair who looked exactly like you."

"I thought it was you at first, Mr. Hudson," Benny said. "But then I realized that the man was too..." Benny paused.

"Messy." Francis finished the sentence.

"Yes," Benny agreed, his face coloring. "Mr. Hudson is always dressed so neatly."

"We may look alike," Francis said, "but other than that we are as different as brothers can be."

"We are very different," Mr. Hudson agreed. "And I'm sorry to say that it led to quite a few fights when we were younger."

"I'm sorry about those fights, Charles," Francis said.

# Caught!

"I am too." Mr. Hudson looked at the Aldens. "Francis and I loved each other, but we disagreed about many things."

"Charles was fussy and neat," Francis said. "His half of the room was always clean and organized. I was a lot a messier, and I drove him crazy sometimes."

Mr. Hudson smiled. "And Francis was a great athlete, but I couldn't even run without tripping over my own two feet. Francis liked to go to sleep early, especially before big games, while I liked to stay up late reading. He used to be so annoyed with me for keeping the light on."

Both brothers laughed at the memories.

"After our parents died, we fought a lot more often," Francis said.

"I wanted you to stay in school and get a good education," Mr. Hudson remembered.

Francis nodded. "And I wanted to quit school and work in my friend's carpentry shop. One day, after a particularly big fight, I got very angry and left home without a word. Since then, I've traveled all around the country. I've lived and worked in many different states. My life has been very interesting. But throughout all those years, I always missed my home and my brother."

"Why didn't you call or write?" asked Mr. Hudson. "I always wondered where you were."

"I thought you might not want me back," Francis explained. "I know that I was quite a troublemaker. I was afraid that we would just start fighting again. Then, a few months ago, I finally decided to take the risk and come back and see you. The older I've gotten, the more I've realized how much my family and my old home mean to me. I was going to surprise you. But when I saw the sign on the lawn that said that the house was for sale, I became angry. You weren't ever supposed to sell this house, Charles. Our parents wanted us to keep it in the family as long as we were alive. But I had been gone for so long. I knew I couldn't demand anything from you."

"So you decided to scare away the people who came to buy the house?" Henry asked.

"Yes." Francis hung his head. "I admit it. I pretended to haunt the graveyard at night. I wore a cape, and I even sprinkled fake blood on tombstones and people's back porches. I tried to do all the things that the vampire did in the stories you used to tell me when we were growing up. I knew it would start people talking and word would get around. I thought that no one would want to buy a house with a vampire in the backyard."

Henry pulled a small vial from his pocket. "Was this the blood that you used?"

"Yes!" Francis exclaimed. "But it is only colored water. Where did you find that?"

"You dropped it when we bumped into each other at the library fair," Benny explained. "I tried to catch you to give it back, but you ran away."

"I was worried when you called me 'Mr. Hudson,'" Francis said. "I thought you might know who I was. I didn't want Charles to know I was in town until I had finished scaring away all the buyers for the house."

"Did you take *The Legend of the Vampire* from my backpack?" asked Benny.

"I did," Francis said. "I saw you put it in there on that first day that you met my brother. I needed more ideas for my vampire haunting. I knew I could find them in the book."

"And then you left the picture in the book," Jessie added.

"Yes. I was so surprised to see young Benny there at the diner, that I jumped up and left, leaving the book behind. Imagine how surprised I was to find the book on the kitchen table later that night."

"That's because I left it there by accident." Benny sighed.

"I figured as much," Francis said. "The flowers were replanted, and the porch was scrubbed. I knew you kids had been here."

"You wrote those terrible words in ink on our front porch?" Charles asked. "How could you do that?"

Francis looked sheepish. "I'm very sorry, Charles. I promise to repaint the porch for you. I was only trying to be a good vampire. But I suppose I didn't do a very good job of it. The Aldens came back to the house at night. I thought they would be too frightened for that."

"We were looking for the book," Benny explained.

# Caught!

"I knew Charles had gone out of town, and so I took the key from under the pot. We always kept it there, even when we were children. I was having a nice sandwich and reading by flashlight when you children surprised me. I rushed into the basement. When I heard footsteps on the stairs, I had to quickly sneak out the back door. I circled around to the front. I thought I could get back in to get the rest of my sandwich and the book, but these two kids where standing by the door." Francis pointed at Violet and Benny.

"You tried to scare us with a bat," Benny said.

Francis chuckled. He put his two hands together and flapped his fingers as though they were wings. "Remember this, Charles? We used to make all kinds of animal shapes in the shadows at night. I was quite good at it."

"You still are!" Violet said. "It looked very much like a real bat. We were frightened."

Mr. Hudson shook his head. "Francis, I wish you hadn't done all these things. I wish you had just come and talked to me."

Francis sighed. "I know that now. And I'm

sorry." Francis turned to Violet. "I apologize for frightening you."

"And where did you put all the 'For Sale' signs that you stole?" asked Mr. Hudson. "You have to return them to Josh. You upset him as well."

Francis looked confused.

"Your brother didn't steal the 'For Sale' signs," Violet said. "Josh did that."

"What?" Mr. Hudson turned to look at his Realtor. "Why would Josh steal his own signs? That doesn't make any sense. He wants to sell the house. It's his job."

Josh stuck his hands even deeper into his pockets. He seemed to be trying to find something to say.

"Josh has a friend who wants your house, Mr. Hudson," Violet explained. "Only he can't afford to buy it unless you lower the price. Josh didn't start the vampire rumors, but he helped them along. He thought that if buyers were frightened away, you would be happy to sell the house for a lot less money to his friend. I saw the missing 'For Sale' signs in the back of Josh's car, and I overheard him on the phone with his friend."

Josh's face was bright red. "You should know that it is not right to eavesdrop!" he shouted at Violet.

"I was not eavesdropping!" Violet crossed her arms and stood her ground. "I was working in the garden when you made a call near the front porch. I couldn't help but hear what you said."

"And you should know that you were supposed to be working for me and not for your friend," Mr. Hudson added. "You're fired as my Realtor, Josh."

Josh bit hard on his lower lip. He took a few steps toward the door, then turned back around. "I'm very sorry, Charles," he said. "And I'm sorry for accusing you, Violet. My friend doesn't have a lot of money, and he has five children. I thought this would be the perfect house for him. But it was wrong of me to try to ruin your chances of selling at a good price. I didn't mean any harm, but I know what I did was wrong. I hope you'll forgive me."

Josh pushed open the screen door to leave just as Mrs. Fairfax was about to knock.

"What is going on over here?" she complained, stepping into the living room. "All this commotion has got to stop. Realtors, children, police cars. What next?"

"Hello, Martha," said Francis.

"Francis? Is that Francis?" Mrs. Fairfax put her hand over her heart.

Mr. Hudson helped Mrs. Fairfax into a seat. "It's my brother all right, Martha," he said with a smile. "He's come back to live with me."

"So you're not selling the house?" Mrs. Fairfax asked.

Mr. Hudson looked at his brother and paused. "No, I'm not selling. That is," he continued, "as long as Francis agrees to move in and help me out with the house."

Francis stood and threw his arm around his brother's shoulder. "Thank you, Charles," he said. "There is nothing I would like better. It is so good to be home!"

Suddenly, a loud growling noise came from the sofa. Everyone turned to look.

Benny's face turned bright red. He clasped his hands over his stomach. "Excuse me," he apologized.

# Caught!

Everyone laughed, even Mrs. Fairfax.

"I suppose tracking down vampires can make a person quite hungry." Mr. Hudson smiled.

"*Everything* makes Benny hungry," Henry explained.

Mr. Hudson brought out a pitcher of lemonade and set a tray of snacks on the table for his company.

Everyone was excited when Mr. Hudson told them that the producers had agreed to film the movie version of *The Legend of the Vampire*. It was going to be set right in Greenfield.

"Maybe we can all have a role in the film!" Benny cried.

"That would be so exciting," Jessie agreed. "At the very least, perhaps we can come and watch the filming. Would that be all right with you, Mr. Hudson?"

"Of course!" Mr. Hudson said. "You are more than welcome."

"Are you going to write any more books, Mr. Hudson?" Violet asked.

"I never stop writing, Violet," Mr. Hudson said. "And I'm always looking for ideas for my next story."

As Benny reached for a third helping of cheese and crackers, his stomach let out another loud growl.

Mr. Hudson laughed. "Maybe my next book could be called *The Legend of the Bottomless Stomach*."

"And if that book is made into a movie, I could have the lead role!" Benny grinned. "I knew my stomach would make me famous!"

THE BOXCAR CHILDREN ®

BOOK
144

CREATED BY
GERTRUDE
CHANDLER
WARNER

# HIDDEN IN THE HAUNTED SCHOOL

ILLUSTRATED BY
ANTHONY VanARSDALE

# Contents

# CHAPTER

1

# Ghost Stories

*Crunch!* Benny Alden took a big bite out of his crisp, red apple as he sat in the backseat of the family's minivan. It was a late-fall Saturday, and he and his brother and sisters had helped their grandfather run errands in Silver City, the town next to Greenfield. They'd made a lot of stops, including at the farmers' market. Benny, who was six years old and always hungry, was munching on his second apple, which he'd retrieved from one of the bags of fresh fruits and vegetables tucked near his seat. Now it was late afternoon, and the Aldens were headed home.

Twelve-year-old Jessie put her hand on the cool glass of the minivan's window. She watched trees

221

with red, orange, and yellow leaves whiz by. She thought the leaves looked even prettier than usual in the setting sun. Just then, she remembered the notebook in her backpack. She pulled it out and opened it to check the list of errands they'd made that day. She liked making lists and used her organizational skills to help her family.

"Grandfather," Jessie called to the front seat. "I think we forgot to pick up the dry cleaning."

"You're right!" her grandfather replied. He clicked on the turn signal and turned the van down a side street. "It's a bit out of the way, but I think I know a shortcut to the cleaners."

Benny looked around the minivan.

"I don't think we have room for one more thing," he said. "It's crowded in here!" He was sitting next to Violet, his ten-year-old sister, who was busy doodling with her favorite purple pen in her sketch pad. They were surrounded by bags and boxes holding everything the Aldens had bought or picked up on their errands.

"We'll make room," Henry told his little brother. At fourteen, Henry was the oldest of the Alden children. He sat in the front seat, tinkering with the radio. "Watch can sit on your lap!"

Watch, the Aldens' terrier, replied with a small yap—as if he knew everyone was talking about him. They all laughed as the dog jumped into Benny's lap and curled into a ball.

A few miles and a couple of turns later, the minivan drove down a narrow road that ran along the edge of town. The street was very quiet. The children didn't see any other cars, just rows and rows of trees in the woods on either side of them.

"What's that?" Benny asked, pointing out his window. The Alden children turned to see an old brick building surrounded by a black iron fence. The fence had spiked posts, and overgrown vines hung from the roof. Henry looked beyond the locked gate to read the letters carved into the stone above the entrance.

"Hawthorne School," he said. "I've heard stories about it."

The dark shadows behind the school's broken windows made Violet shiver in her seat.

A few minutes later, Grandfather drove the

minivan into the lot of Silver City Plaza, a shopping center with half a dozen stores. The spots in front of the dry cleaning shop were full, so he parked in front of Weaver's Flower Shop.

"I'll be right back," he told his grandchildren.

Grandfather had been gone only a moment when Benny spoke up. "Tell us about Hawthorne School," he said to his brother. "It looks spooky."

"Do you mean Haunted School?" Henry asked. "That's what they call it."

"Why?" Violet asked. Although she certainly thought the school looked haunted.

"Well, it's been abandoned since the 1950s," Henry said. "The gates haven't been opened since the day it closed."

"That doesn't make it haunted," Violet pointed out.

"Of course not," Jessie agreed. "But now that you mention it, wasn't the ghost story we heard last weekend about this school?"

Last weekend, Grandfather had treated Henry, Jessie, and a few of their friends to a campfire. Violet and Benny had stayed in the house to

watch a movie with Mrs. McGregor. As the group sat around the small fire pit, they roasted marshmallows and exchanged their scariest ghost stories. Jessie's friend, Rose, had told everyone the tale of a haunted school—a school that she said was nearby. It had to be Hawthorne School.

Henry nodded. "I remember. The story says the ghost of the former principal still walks the halls of the school."

"A *ghost*?" Benny asked.

"That's right," Jessie said, recalling the story. "She was fired from her job because a teacher reported that she was stealing money from the school. After weeks of insisting she didn't do it, the principal was still told to leave. As she walked out of the building, she put a curse on the school!"

"The money was later found," Henry continued. "It turns out she didn't steal it after all."

"Did she get her job back?" Benny asked.

"No," Jessie replied. "Nobody could find her after she was asked to leave. She seemed to just... vanish."

"Now," Henry added, "if you look through the

old windows, you can see her walking back and forth through the halls. Or that's what they say, at least."

"Wow!" Benny exclaimed.

"A real ghost!" Violet said.

"We don't really believe the story," Henry said. "It's probably just a local legend."

The Alden children looked at one another, deep in thought. They heard the clicking sound of the door being unlocked and turned their attention back to Grandfather. He had returned from the dry cleaners with an armload of plastic-covered shirts.

"Look what I found," he said, climbing into the minivan. He handed a yellow piece of paper to Jessie. "You might want to consider this for service work."

Jessie read the paper. She smiled and handed it to Henry.

"Volunteers needed," he read aloud. "Thanks, Grandfather!"

Henry and Jessie's middle school required them to work ten hours of community service every year. In return, they received extra credit. They both enjoyed helping in the neighborhood and meeting new people, and they were looking for new places to volunteer.

"I was thinking about helping the teachers at Greenfield Day Care Center," Jessie said as Grandfather started the car on the journey home. "They can always use an extra pair of hands."

"And the Rec Center is looking for junior camp leaders," Henry added. "Taking little kids on adventures would be fun!"

Benny looked out the window and into the woods as they drove past them again. He thought about his own exciting adventure.

Years ago, the children's parents had died, leaving them without a home. They knew they had a grandfather but had never met him, and they had heard he was mean. So, when they thought they would be sent to live with him, they ran away into the woods. There they found an old boxcar, which they made their home. They found their dog, Watch, while they were living in the boxcar. When Grandfather finally discovered the children, they learned he was actually a very kind man. He loved them very much.

They became a family, and Grandfather moved their boxcar into the backyard of their home in Greenfield so they could use it as a clubhouse.

"I wish I could help with the little kids," Benny said. The Aldens laughed, since Benny was not much older than the campers.

"It would be great to find a place where we could all work together," Jessie added.

"Any other ideas?" Grandfather asked.

The Aldens were quiet for a moment as they tried to think of places where they could all volunteer as a family.

Suddenly Violet gasped. "Stop!" she cried. "Look!"

Grandfather pulled the car over to the side of the road.

"What's the matter, Violet?" he asked.

They were sitting in front of Hawthorne School.

Violet pointed a shaky finger out the window.

"The door to the school is open!" she exclaimed. "It wasn't before!"

The Aldens peered out to see that the iron gate of the old school was wide open. And so was the front door!

"I thought the school has been locked up since it closed," Benny said.

"It has been," Henry replied.

The siblings looked at the old school. The sun was setting behind the trees, casting a long shadow across the front of the building. In the darkness, the children could clearly see a flickering light in one of the upstairs windows.

"Is someone in there?" Violet asked. "Is this school really haunted?"

# CHAPTER 2

# The Old Becomes New

"Well, would you look at that," Grandfather marveled. "Nobody's been in that place for over fifty years. I wonder what's happening."

"Do you think it's haunted?" Benny asked.

"I saw a light flickering!" Violet said.

"So did I," Jessie added. "Look through the upstairs window!"

Through the window, everyone saw a dim flicker of light. Then, the school went dark again.

"Wait," said Henry. "I think I know what's going on."

He unfolded the yellow piece of paper that Grandfather had given them. "I saw something on this flyer, and now it all makes sense." He read the flyer over before reading it aloud.

"'Volunteers needed,'" he began. "'For a renovation project and cleanup at the new Hawthorne Art Center.'"

"That's right," Grandfather said, scratching his chin. "I remember reading something about this in the *Greenfield Gazette*. Silver City has been planning to fix up an old building for their art center. They must have picked the old Hawthorne School."

"A community art center?" Violet asked. "I wonder what art programs they'll offer." She motioned for Jessie to hand her the flyer. "Art and dance classes," she read aloud from the paper. "And, they will have a theater for plays and music recitals!"

"What a nice addition to Silver City," Grandfather said.

"I really want to know more!" Jessie agreed.

Henry looked up at the old school, imagining how the building would look when it was fixed up. He noticed a rusty blue pickup in the school's parking lot. The truck had a ladder and a big toolbox in the back. *Silver City Electric* was written on the truck's side in silver letters. Henry pointed it out to his siblings.

"That truck looks familiar," he said.

"As a matter of fact, that's my old friend Bob's truck," Grandfather told them. "Remember when he fixed the lights at our house? He's an electrician here in town."

"That's right," Henry said. "Will he know about the restoration project?"

"We should ask him!" Violet said. As shy as she was, she was the one who was the most excited about the new art center.

"Sure," Grandfather replied. "I've known Bob for years. It will be good to catch up with him."

"Do you think the school is as creepy on the inside as it is on the outside?" Jessie asked.

"I hope so!" Benny said.

Jessie slid the minivan door open.

"Come on, Watch!" Benny called. Watch trotted happily alongside the Aldens as they made their way past the iron fence and gate.

As they approached the stone front steps, Bob stepped into the doorway and waved. "Hello!" he called.

He wore a blue and silver T-shirt with *Silver City Electric* on it and carried a flashlight. He stepped out onto the stairs and closed the school door behind him.

Grandfather waved back. "Hi, Bob! We saw your truck. Do you remember my grandchildren?"

Bob greeted Henry, Jessie, Violet, and Benny, giving each a friendly handshake. Suddenly, the school's door swung open with a loud *clank*. A young man appeared. He was wearing a T-shirt like Bob's. His sandy-brown hair matched Bob's too. He held a large camera that hung from a brown leather strap around his neck.

"There you are, Ansel," Bob said to the young man. "I must have lost you inside." He introduced the young man as his son. Ansel gave them a quick wave before turning away and fiddling with his camera.

"We must've seen your flashlight!" Henry said. He remembered the light they saw flickering in the window.

"I'm sure you did," Bob replied. "Ansel and I just stopped by to look at the old place. I'm overseeing the renovation project and need to make sure it's safe for our volunteers. The inside isn't too bad, just needs a little elbow grease."

Jessie's eyes grew wide, and so did her smile. "Bob," she started. "Are you still looking for volunteers?"

"We'd love to help," Violet added. She didn't want to miss an opportunity to work on the new art center.

"We sure could use volunteers," Bob replied. "We'd love for every one of you to pitch in." He nodded to all of the Alden children.

"Can you tell me more about the project?" Grandfather asked.

He then pulled Bob aside to ask about the specific jobs his grandchildren would be doing.

While Grandfather and Bob were talking, Ansel was still busy with his camera, staring at the digital screen. He carefully studied each photo as he clicked through them.

"Will you also be working here, Ansel?" Henry asked.

"I'm on the arts committee," Ansel replied,

though he didn't look up from his camera. "So, I'll be around."

"Let's look inside," Benny suggested. He pointed to the grand door of the school. "Just a peek!"

"First," Henry said, "let's ask Bob if it's safe."

Grandfather gave his approval with a brief thumbs-up gesture.

"Grandfather agrees with Bob," Henry said. "The structure is safe."

"Let's go!" Benny said.

Henry opened the school's door. Jessie found a large stone and propped the door open with it.

"Come on, Watch!" she called.

Inside, Violet instantly noticed a trophy case. It was covered with a layer of soot, dust, and grime. A few trophies remained in the case. Through the dirty glass, Violet saw a tall, tarnished old cup. On another shelf, smaller trophies were draped in cobwebs. She frowned.

"At one time," she said, pointing to the trophies, "these were shiny and new."

The Aldens continued walking along the dark hallway.

# The Old Becomes New

"Check this out," Jessie said. She was peering at a framed black-and-white photo hanging on the wall. The picture was faded and torn around the edges. The students in the picture wore dark, formal clothes. The date *March 14, 1920* was scribbled on the bottom. Jessie recorded the date in her notebook.

"They're not smiling," Henry noted.

"I don't think it was fashionable to smile in pictures back then," Jessie replied.

Benny followed his sisters and brother as they walked into a classroom. The first thing he noticed was a large clock on the wall behind an old teacher's desk. The clock's hands had stopped with the hour hand pointing to twelve and the minute hand to three. Benny shuddered. He wondered how long ago the clock's hands had stopped turning.

"This place is definitely as creepy on the inside as the outside!" he exclaimed.

Rows of smaller desks sat across from the teacher's desk. Jessie lifted one of the desks' tops. Inside, she found broken pencils and old papers. Shifting through the papers, Violet found an old cloth doll. The doll's hair was made of yellow yarn, and its clothes were faded fabric scraps. A small button had been sewn on for an eye, but the other eye's button was missing.

"This place *is* spooky," Violet said. "We'd better get back. Grandfather might be looking for us."

When the Aldens returned to the front steps, Grandfather was still talking with Bob.

"Good news," Grandfather said. "Volunteers start next week."

"We'll get this place looking brand-new!" Bob said.

"Sure," Ansel muttered.

He kept his head down, but it looked to Jessie like he was trying to hide a scowl.

She wondered why Ansel wasn't more excited to be a part of the project. After all, it was an art center, and he clearly loved taking photos.

"We're going to grab the volunteer paperwork from the truck," Grandfather said. He and Bob headed toward the parking lot.

While they all waited, Ansel sighed. He looked unhappy.

Jessie tried to break the ice. "Are you excited about the new art center?"

Ansel looked up. Then he turned and gazed up at the old school. His eyes narrowed. "This place should be kept the way it is," he said bitterly. And with that, he marched off to the parking lot.

"What was that about?" Henry asked.

Jessie shrugged. "I don't know," she said.

"I want to see the swings!" Benny said just then. He had noticed the rusty playground equipment near the front fence. "Can we wait for Grandfather on the playground?"

"Sure," Jessie said. "But be careful." They walked over to the broken-down playground. Violet and Benny sat on the swings, which creaked and screeched as they moved back and forth. They faced the school yard where the grass and shrubs were overgrown. Long vines wrapped around the fence. The untended yard added to the creepiness of the school.

Henry walked around looking at the old seesaws, while Jessie sat still on one of the swings. She was thinking about Ansel's odd behavior. Her thoughts were interrupted by Watch's loud bark, which startled her.

"What's with Watch?" Benny asked. The dog had tensed up, and now he nervously paced in front of the children. Then he stopped and growled in the direction of the school.

"It feels like...like someone is watching us," Jessie said.

Benny looked at the dark windows of the old school. "There's no such thing as ghosts," he said aloud. "Right?"

# CHAPTER 3

# An Important Lesson

It was the first day of volunteer work.

"See you in a few hours!" Grandfather called from the minivan. He waved to the children as they climbed the front steps of Hawthorne School.

Jessie stopped for a moment to look up at the old building. In the morning daylight, Jessie couldn't remember what about the place had her so nervous just a week ago.

"Hawthorne School doesn't look so spooky today," Violet said. She was thinking the same thing as her sister.

So was Henry, who gazed at the tower on the top of the school. It looked majestic against the clear, sunny sky.

## An Important Lesson

Today the school wasn't deserted at all. Two dozen volunteers had come to help clean up the building. Benny thought all the people looked like a swarm of worker ants. Some were carrying buckets and brooms. They busily swept the sidewalks and stairs. Other volunteers had paintbrushes tucked into their back pockets. Henry stepped off the sidewalk to let two men carrying a faded sofa go by. He had moved just in time. Two more volunteers went by carrying an old rolled-up rug.

The inside of the school was just as busy. A team of teens from the high school was washing the thick grime from the windows. Nearby, a group of women was scraping the windowsills clean to prepare them for a fresh coat of paint.

After a few minutes, the Aldens found Bob at the volunteer check-in table. He checked their names off a long list and then gave the children their assignments.

"Benny and Violet," Bob said. "You will be helping hand out water and snacks at the snack tent on the front lawn."

"Perfect!" Benny exclaimed.

"Just don't eat all the snacks," Violet added. Everyone laughed, including Benny.

Bob turned to Henry and Jessie. "You'll be sweeping and dusting classrooms today."

"Great," Henry said.

Meanwhile Jessie looked around and noticed a large sign in the corner that said AUCTION. She was curious.

"What's the auction?" she asked Bob.

"The volunteers will bring the old furniture up here." He pointed to the corner. "We'll evaluate it. And then we'll sell it in an auction. The money we make will cover some of the renovation costs."

Everyone agreed an auction was a great idea. They headed back outside and found the snack table. It was set up under a large, blue tent. Benny and Violet went to work placing bottles of water on a table.

"We'll be right inside," Jessie told them.

Henry and Jessie stopped to pick up brooms and dusting cloths before heading back into the school. After sweeping the main hallway, they started working in one of the old classrooms.

Henry pulled a cloth out of his back pocket.

# An Important Lesson

With a swipe of his hand, he removed a thick layer of grime from a window. When he finished one window, he moved on to the next one.

"It will take some elbow grease to get these windows clean," he said.

Jessie wrinkled her nose as she used her broom to pull a stringy cobweb from the corner. Then she swept a big pile of dust bunnies into a dustpan. She was finishing up when a young woman walked into the classroom. The woman had dark hair with bangs that fell into her eyes.

"Hi," Jessie said, walking over to her. "I'm Jessie. And this is my brother, Henry."

"Hello," the woman replied. "I'm Martha."

Martha immediately began to follow Jessie and Henry around the room with a cloth rag in her hand. Every once in a while, she wiped the rag over the top of a desk or along the seat of a chair.

Henry noticed that Martha was missing spots. She seemed to be focused on studying the furniture, rather than dusting it. He watched her lift a chair and inspect the bottom of it. She even examined the legs of a table.

"These chairs are in good shape for being so old," Martha muttered.

Henry agreed. "Will you be working here all weekend?" he asked.

Martha seemed a little flustered by his question.

"Yes," she replied. "I'll be here with you and your brother and sisters. How's your little dog, Watch? Is he here today too?"

"No," Henry replied. "He's at home."

Jessie was still sweeping when she overheard Martha talking with Henry. She wondered how Martha knew their dog's name. Jessie was certain that this was their first time meeting her.

But before she had a chance to ask Martha about it, another woman wandered into the room. Her gray hair was braided and wrapped in a bun. She wore glasses on a chain around her neck. She took several moments to carefully review the room.

"Did I leave my clipboard in here?" the woman asked. "I'm supposed to be counting the desks and chairs, but I can't seem to find my clipboard."

The woman looked confused.

"We'll help you find it!" Jessie offered.

"Thank you, dear," the woman replied. She lifted her glasses, still glancing around the room. "I'm Mrs. Koslowski. But you can call me Mrs. K."

Jessie and Henry introduced themselves. Then they propped their brooms against the wall. As they walked out of the classroom, Henry turned to Martha.

"It was nice meeting you, Martha," Henry said.

"See you around."

Mumbling a few words of farewell, Martha went back to dusting off a file cabinet.

"Where were you last working?" Henry asked as they walked down the hallway.

"Well, I was in one of the classrooms," Mrs. K replied. "But I can't remember which one."

Just then, Jessie noticed Ansel leaning against the stairwell banister. His eyes were focused on his camera.

"Hello, Ansel!" Mrs. K called. "Have you been here long?"

Ansel looked up and gave a fast wave.

"No," he replied. "Just arrived." And then he went back to looking at his camera. He was no more excited to be here than the day the Aldens had met him.

Henry was surprised that Mrs. K was so forgetful but had remembered Ansel's name. He figured the two had met each other earlier, so he didn't give it much more thought.

As they turned a corner, they heard excited voices coming from down the hall.

## An Important Lesson

"It sounds like something is happening in Room 107," Henry said, pointing to a nearby classroom.

"We better check it out," Jessie replied. "Do you mind if we make a quick stop, Mrs. K?"

Mrs. Koslowski shook her head and followed Jessie and Henry into the room. They saw several volunteers huddled around a chalkboard, along with two of the handymen who were doing the heavier work around the school.

"What's going on?" Jessie asked.

One of the handymen pointed to a large, old bulletin board that had been taken off the wall. "When we removed this," he replied, "we found an even older chalkboard underneath!" He pointed to the chalkboard on the wall. It was clearly much older than the others in the classroom. It had cracks and plaster around the edges, since it had been hidden in the wall underneath the bulletin board. But the most remarkable thing about it was that the chalkboard still had writing and pictures on it!

The handyman explained that some of the classrooms had been redecorated a long time ago.

Many years ago, builders had put up walls and bulletin boards right on top of the old chalkboards. "You know how sometimes in an old house you'll peel back the wallpaper and find older wallpaper underneath? It's a little like that," he said. "We've found old chalkboards in the other rooms, but as you can see, this one is special."

Jessie could see why. The old chalkboard had never been erased after the last time it was used. It was filled with lessons and drawings from nearly one hundred years ago!

"Look at this," Henry exclaimed, pointing to a corner of the chalkboard. "The date is March 20, 1920!"

Everyone gathered around to study the old chalk writing. There was a lesson about a classic poem, which read:

> *How doth the little busy bee*
> *Improve each shining hour,*
> *And gather honey all the day*
> *From every opening flower!*

## An Important Lesson

Henry didn't recognize the poem, but he did admire the old-fashioned cursive handwriting used to write it. Next to the poem was a drawing of a little girl wearing a long dress. It looked like something that would have been stylish many years ago.

Jessie looked at the old arithmetic tables that had been drawn up in one corner. "It's like the students' work has been captured in time!" she marveled.

"This reminds me of my mother's fancy handwriting," Mrs. Koslowski said, coming closer to the chalkboard. "Beautiful penmanship like this isn't taught anymore."

More volunteers came into the classroom as word caught on about the old chalkboard, and they all chatted excitedly about the discovery.

Jessie noticed Ansel walking into the classroom. He snapped a few quick photos, then quietly slipped out of the room.

As he left, Martha strolled in. She looked over the old chalkboard but didn't join in the conversation.

"We should contact the *Silver City Herald*," a young woman suggested. "I'm sure the newspaper will be fascinated by this lesson in history!"

Suddenly, Martha seemed very interested in the volunteers' conversation. She walked over and sat down with the group.

"The newspaper will *not* be interested in this," Martha said. She pulled a notebook from her bag and scribbled down a few notes.

"It's so interesting!" one of the volunteers called out.

"We should not call the local news," Martha repeated.

Jessie watched. She thought that Martha muttered something else under her breath, but she couldn't make out the words. All she knew was that Martha looked irritated. Why? Jessie wondered.

Just then, a red-haired girl ran into the classroom. She looked pale and was out of breath.

"Something's wrong next door!" she said.

CHAPTER
4

# The Locked Door

Jessie and Henry rushed into the hall with the other volunteers. The red-haired girl stood in front of Room 108. With a shaky finger, she pointed to the door.

"What's wrong?" Jessie asked.

The girl's face reddened as she struggled to explain. "I—I was sweeping in there when I realized I forgot my dustpan," she started. "I left the room for just a minute to get it."

She paused to take a deep breath. Jessie could see that the girl was not only baffled, but frightened.

"I heard the door slam shut," the girl continued. "When I came back, the door was locked!"

By now a small crowd had gathered. Even Benny

and Violet had come in from the snack table to see what was going on.

A few volunteers tried to open the door. Benny went over and pulled on the knob too. But the door was definitely locked.

"Maybe the wind blew it closed," suggested one volunteer.

"Or someone else closed and locked the door," offered another.

After a few moments, a woman stepped forward to speak to the crowd. She nervously twirled the cord of her name tag.

"I'm a coordinator on this project," she said. "And I know for a fact that the doors only lock from inside the classroom."

"Is somebody in there?" Henry asked.

"I don't think so," replied the coordinator. "We've got someone bringing a ladder to look in the room and check." She pointed to a small, high window above the door.

The group became noisy as everyone tried to offer explanations for the locked door.

A burly man from the construction crew pushed

through the group carrying a ladder. He smiled as he leaned the ladder against the wall next to the door.

"I'll get to the bottom of this," he said. He climbed the ladder. Then he peered into the small window. By the time he turned to face the group, his smile had faded.

"The room is empty," he said in amazement as he climbed back down the ladder. Then he tested the door to make sure it really was locked. The door remained tightly shut.

Henry exchanged a look with Jessie. Something strange was happening, and they had to see for themselves.

"If you don't mind, may I take a look?" Harry asked the burly man.

"Be my guest," the man replied. "Maybe you'll see something I missed."

Henry climbed up the ladder and peeked through the window. Scanning the room, he realized that nothing unusual stood out. There was definitely nobody in the room, either.

"It's empty," he confirmed.

One of the volunteers gasped in astonishment. Another nervously hugged her arms to her chest.

"Was it a...*ghost* who locked the room?" the red-haired girl asked. "Is the school really haunted?"

The volunteer coordinator stepped forward again.

"It's getting late," she announced. "We'll try to resolve this tomorrow. For now, let's all head home."

Everyone gathered their belongings and shuffled out of the school. On their way out, the volunteers exchanged tales about the Hawthorne ghost. They wondered if the old principal was still walking the halls...and locking classroom doors.

*\*\*\**

"What's going on?" Violet asked. "There are ghost rumors everywhere. Even at the snack tent!"

"Really?" Jessie said.

Violet nodded. "We were handing out water when one of the volunteers asked us about the furniture."

"The furniture?" Henry asked. "What about it?"

"It's been moved!" Benny said.

"That's right," Violet added. "Apparently, some of the furniture was found in the basement."

"And," Benny continued, "nobody knows how it got there."

The Aldens headed toward the parking lot. When they arrived, they spotted Grandfather talking with Bob.

"Bob was just telling me some good news!" Grandfather said when they reached the minivan.

"What's happening?" Violet asked. Everything that involved the art center excited her.

"The arts committee has decided to throw a grand opening party," Bob said. "It's scheduled for six weeks from today. And you are all invited!"

"That's great!" Henry said.

Grandfather nodded. "It's a nice way to let the community know about the new art center."

"It's a tight deadline," Bob said. "But we can do it!"

"Sure!" Grandfather agreed. "Just stay on track, and everything will be ready in time for the party!"

The Aldens climbed into the minivan while discussing the plans for the grand opening. After waving farewell to Bob, Grandfather drove toward Greenfield.

"How was work today?" he asked. "Do you think the art center will be ready in time for the party?"

Violet frowned. She thought about all of the spooky things that had happened that day.

"The school might be haunted," she finally replied.

"Why do you think that?" Grandfather asked.

Violet and the others told him what had happened.

"I'm sure there are reasonable explanations," Grandfather told her.

"I hope it's not haunted," Violet added. "The art center is going to be great!"

As they continued driving, Jessie flipped through the pages of her notebook. She didn't believe in ghosts. But it was clear from her notes that something strange was happening at Hawthorne School. Jessie wondered why Martha had been so irritated when the volunteers mentioned contacting the newspaper. Then there was Room 108. How could the door be locked from the inside when the room was empty?

Benny distracted her from her thoughts. "Something smells good!" he said. He looked around and pulled out a paper bag. WEAVER'S FLOWER AND GARDEN SHOP was written on it in colorful letters. When Benny opened the bag, an aroma of fresh herbs floated into the minivan.

"Weaver's had a special on herbs," Grandfather explained. "I think I'll make my famous spaghetti soon!"

"That is a very good idea!" Benny replied.

Everyone giggled. But as excited as they were about Grandfather's delicious spaghetti, they were also troubled. The day's events had been very unusual. The Aldens rode the rest of the way home in silence. They were busy thinking about how the door to Room 108 could be locked.

\*\*\*

Grandfather dropped them off at Hawthorne School early the next morning. The first thing the children did was go to the door of Room 108. They found volunteers gathered there. Now the door was wide open! Everyone was curious.

# The Locked Door

"Did someone unlock the door?" Benny asked.

"No!" the volunteer coordinator replied. "It was just...open when we got here."

Jessie spotted Martha standing next to Mrs. Koslowski.

"Good morning," Jessie said.

But Martha and Mrs. K didn't hear Jessie. They were too busy discussing the Hawthorne School ghost.

"Do you think it's the ghost of the principal?" Martha asked.

"What if the uncovered chalkboard upset her?" Mrs. K continued.

"We shouldn't have moved anything," another volunteer added.

"I also heard that furniture has been turning up in odd places," another volunteer continued. "Bob said that some of the old desks were in the basement."

"Really?" Martha asked. "Bob noticed the furniture had been moved?"

"Yes," the volunteer confirmed. "And he doesn't know how it got there."

Jessie thought Martha had a strange expression on her face. She seemed uneasy, but she didn't say anything else.

"Maybe the locked door was a sign that the Hawthorne ghost doesn't want to be disturbed," Mrs. K suggested.

Jessie stepped back and motioned to her brothers and sister to follow her.

"What's going on?" Violet asked, once they were away from the crowd.

"Let's find a private place to talk," Jessie suggested.

They followed her down the hallway. Just as they turned a corner, they saw a glimpse of a figure quickly ducking into a classroom.

"Was that Ansel?" Henry asked.

"It sure looked like him," Violet said. "Where did he go?"

"Why isn't he helping the volunteers?" Jessie asked.

Henry shrugged.

"He's very mysterious," he replied.

They continued until they reached a set of

swinging double doors.

Jessie peeked through a small crack between the doors.

"It's the gym!" she said. "Let's sit down in here."

Benny swung open the doors and rushed through them.

"Wow," he said. "I've never been in here before."

The gym floor was grubby and strewn with old leaves that had blown in through one of the broken windows, but even so, the Aldens could see the gym floor still had some of its old shine. Instead of being spooky, the big room was bright and pleasant, with the sunlight coming through the grimy skylights overhead.

"It's just like our gym at school!" Jessie exclaimed. "Only dustier."

"That's for sure," Henry said.

Tattered nets hung from the basketball hoops. The scoreboard looked broken, and the leather mats hanging along the wall were stiff and cracked. Paint peeled from the bleachers, which looked too rickety to sit on. But there was a pair of low, sturdy benches by the door.

"Let's sit down," Jessie suggested.

The Aldens sat facing one another on the wood benches.

"Something strange is definitely happening around here," Jessie said. "Did you hear about the desks that showed up in the basement? A couple of the volunteers were talking about them."

"Maybe Bob moved them?" Henry suggested.

"That's the thing," Jessie continued. "I just heard the volunteers say that Bob doesn't know how they got there. Nobody does."

Violet shivered. "Everyone thinks it's the ghost, don't they?"

"Well," Jessie said. "Martha looked upset when she heard about the furniture in the basement. But I'm not sure what that means."

"Maybe it means she believes in the Hawthorne School ghost," Violet said.

"But there's no such thing as ghosts," Benny said. "Right?"

"Right!" Henry replied.

"So who's causing all of the strange things to happen?" Benny asked.

# The Locked Door

"That's what we have to figure out," Henry replied.

The children looked around the gym. Even though it wasn't spooky like the rest of the school, there were so many unanswered questions.

Henry stood up. "Let's get to work," he suggested. "There's still a lot to do before the grand opening."

"And today, we have granola bars at the snack tent!" Benny added.

Everyone laughed as they got up and walked out of the gym. When they were back in the hallway, Jessie stopped to face her brothers and sister.

"There may not be a ghost," she said. "But we should all keep an eye out for anything unusual."

As they were about to head to their jobs, they head a sharp cry that stopped them short. The noise had come from above them.

"What was *that*?" Violet asked.

"That," Jessie said, "was a scream!"

# CHAPTER

5

# A Mysterious Warning

"Let's go," Henry said. He pointed to the floor above them. "It's coming from upstairs!"

When the Aldens reached the second floor, they heard voices coming from Room 214. They went into the room, where a group of volunteers— including Martha and Mrs. K—were talking nervously. A few of the volunteers looked pale and frightened.

"What's going on?" Henry asked. "We heard someone scream."

The volunteers were huddled in the front of the classroom. Martha stepped aside so the Alden children could see the chalkboard. She waved at it, motioning for them to step forward for a closer

266

look. When they did, they saw a message written on it. The cursive handwriting looked very much like the writing found on the old hidden chalkboard in Room 107. The same fancy handwriting that Mrs. K had admired.

"What does it mean?" Jessie asked. She opened her notebook and wrote down the exact words of the message.

*Stay away! Whoever dares unlock my secret will be sorry!*

She wondered who would send such a warning.

"When I was working in here earlier, the chalkboard was blank!" Martha explained. She took a few deep breaths before she continued. "I stepped away for just a few minutes to get a bottle of water from the snack tent. When I returned...I saw the message!"

Martha shivered.

"It must be the ghost," she said nervously.

One of the volunteers, an older lady with graying curls, was also visibly shaken by the eerie message. She stared at the chalkboard and blinked several times. She seemed to be trying to convince herself

that she was really seeing the strange words.

"The legend must be true," she finally said. "The Hawthorne School ghost doesn't want us here!"

For a few more moments, she continued to gaze at the chalkboard. And then suddenly, she began collecting her bags and belongings.

"I'm not sticking around to find out what's going on here," she said as she slipped on her jacket. Swinging her bag over her shoulder, she marched out of the classroom.

A short woman with blond hair had been watching the group. She abruptly stood up from her chair. "I think I'll join her," she said. She gave an apologetic glance as she left the room.

Another volunteer started to gather his belongings. "I don't believe in ghosts," he said. "But this is very strange!" He rushed out the door.

The Alden children looked at one another. If many more volunteers left, the art center wouldn't be finished in time for the grand opening. Everyone seemed shaken by the message. But the Aldens knew that time was ticking. They had to find out who was behind this...and fast!

"I'm sure a ghost isn't responsible for this message," Jessie said. She remembered her grandfather's advice. "There must be a reasonable answer."

She looked over at the remaining volunteers, who were still staring at the message and talking among themselves. Martha looked uneasy. She put a hand against the wall to steady herself, and Jessie thought that she might faint.

"Are you OK?" Jessie asked. She jumped out of her seat so Martha could sit down.

"Thanks," Martha replied. "Would you mind handing me my bottle of water? It's over there in my bag." She pointed to a large leather tote bag sitting on the window ledge.

"Sure," Jessie said. She went over to the bag and looked inside. There she saw a box of business cards that had accidentally opened up. A dozen identical bright-green cards had spilled out and were scattered all throughout the bag. Jessie could see they were Martha's business cards, and as she pulled out the water bottle, she couldn't help but read one that was facing up.

# A Mysterious Warning

Jessie quickly closed the bag, then went over to Martha and handed her the water.

"Thank you," Martha replied, still sounding a little upset.

"I hope you feel better," Jessie told her.

Martha managed a small smile.

Jessie went back over to her brothers and sister. They needed to talk about the strange message on the board.

"Follow me," she whispered to her siblings, as they all left Room 214 and quietly closed the door.

"Do you think a ghost is really haunting these classrooms?" Violet asked as soon as they were out in the hallway.

Jessie was about to reply when the door opened behind them. They turned to see Martha leaving the classroom. She still had a strange look on her face and was walking quickly. As she slung her tote bag over her shoulder, a small piece of paper fell out, but she didn't stop. Jessie ran to pick it up, but by the time she had it in her hand, Martha had turned a corner. She was out of sight before Jessie could call to her.

Jessie looked down at the piece of paper. It was one of the bright-green business cards she had seen in Martha's bag.

"What is it?" Violet asked.

Jessie tucked the card into her back pocket and looked at her sister and brothers. "I'm not sure yet, but I'll show you over lunch. It's time for our break, isn't it?"

"It sure is," said Henry, checking his watch.

"I knew it was time for lunch even without a watch," Benny said, rubbing his tummy.

Violet checked the backpack she was carrying that held their food. Mrs. McGregor had made them each a brown bag lunch.

"I have an idea!" she said. "Let's find the lunchroom in this school! There has to be one, right? We can eat our sandwiches there, just like kids did in the old days."

Before long, they had found a door with a sign that said CAFETERIA.

The lunchroom looked a little bit like the one from the Aldens' own school. But the walls were covered in faded posters from the 1950s, showing black-and-white pictures of food. Jessie stood in front of a picture of a sandwich cut into neat triangles.

"It's a...cream cheese and pickle sandwich?" she said. She raised her eyebrows. "Yikes!"

The pickles in the picture were gray, and they didn't look very good to Jessie.

"I don't know," said Henry. "That sounds delicious! Except I would want olives instead of pickles."

"Really?" said Violet. "I can't imagine! The food was really weird in the fifties. Look!" She pointed to an old bulletin board with a tattered menu pinned to it.

"Today's lunch," she read aloud. "Milk, minced meat, mashed potatoes, beet relish, and tapioca pudding."

"*Beet* relish?" Benny asked. He wrinkled his nose. "I'm glad Mrs. McGregor made our lunch!" All the same, he was fascinated by the old menu and made Violet read the whole thing to him.

They sat down at one of the long tables. Benny opened his bag and let the contents spill out. He smiled when he saw Mrs. McGregor's famous turkey sandwich. She also had added carrots and a little tub of peanut butter. "My favorite!" Benny cheered, when he discovered the freshly baked chocolate-chip cookies.

The group was silent while they ate their sandwiches. Then Jessie pulled the small card from her pocket and stared at it.

"This is Martha's business card," she said. "I saw it in her bag when I got her water bottle. And...I think it's a clue!"

"What do you mean?" Henry asked.

"Well," Jessie replied, "the card says that Martha sells antique furniture! She has her own business."

"That would explain why she was looking at the desks so closely," Henry said. He remembered the first time they had met Martha.

"Wow," Violet said. "This school is filled with old furniture."

"Yes," Jessie continued. "I think Martha has been more interested in the furniture than in the restoration project. She must be looking for antiques to sell."

# A Mysterious Warning

"Maybe *she* was the one who moved those desks into the basement," Henry said.

"And if she moved the furniture, then the Hawthorne School ghost didn't do it!" Bennie added.

"Exactly!" Jessie agreed.

Violet frowned. "That all makes sense," she said. "But why didn't Martha just tell us she was looking for antiques? Why all the sneaking around?"

Jessie crossed her arms and sighed. "That's a good question."

"And another thing," Violet added. "How did Martha know Watch's name?"

# CHAPTER 6

# Unusual Business

That evening, Grandfather made his famous spaghetti. He had spent an hour standing over the bubbling pot of sauce before he left it to simmer on the stove. Each time one of the children entered the kitchen to offer their help, he shooed them away. "It's a secret recipe!" he would say.

After dinner they made tapioca pudding for dessert. Benny had given Mrs. McGregor the idea after the Aldens returned from Hawthorne School. Benny told her all about the old menu. When he mentioned tapioca pudding, Mrs. McGregor took out a cookbook and showed him a picture of what looked like vanilla pudding filled with tiny, round blobs. Benny thought the pudding looked really funny, but he wanted to try it.

Now Mrs. McGregor set out the ingredients so the children could help make it. She showed them the package of tapioca, which looked like little white beads.

"Tapioca comes from the root of a South American plant called cassava," she explained.

"I think I've had tapioca before," Jessie said. "I had some bubble tea at the mall once, and there were little round pieces in it! They were soft, like jelly. It was weird but good!"

"Wow!" Benny said. Mrs. McGregor let him pour the beads into a measuring cup while she heated the milk for the pudding in a saucepan. Jessie cracked two eggs into a bowl and whisked them together.

"Violet," Mrs. McGregor said, "will you get the sugar, vanilla, and salt?"

After a few minutes, Mrs. McGregor added the rest of the ingredients to the milk. Each of the Aldens took turns slowly stirring the mixture.

"Is it done?" Benny asked. He looked at the creamy pudding. It was now thick and filled with little translucent globes of tapioca.

"I think so," Mrs. McGregor told him. She poured the pudding into a bowl and covered it with wax paper. Benny opened the refrigerator door, and Mrs. McGregor set the sweet pudding inside.

While they waited for the pudding to cool, Mrs. McGregor finished cleaning the kitchen and Grandfather went to read in the next room. Benny, Jessie, and Violet gathered around Henry while he showed them what he'd found online.

"I wanted to know more about Martha's antique business," he said. "So I went to the website listed on her business card."

Benny pointed to a photo on the screen. "Those look like desks from Hawthorne School."

"They sure do," Henry said. "'Original antiques from a historic Silver City building,'" he read aloud. "'Will be in stock soon. No other dealer in town has these unique desks!'"

"Hmm," Violet said. "'No other dealer in town.' Do you think Martha has been making the school seem haunted so that nobody else would find out about those old desks?"

"It's a good theory," Jessie agreed. "She didn't

want anyone to know she was interested in the desks. And she definitely didn't want other antique dealers to know about the school."

"That must be why she didn't want anyone to call the newspaper when we found the lesson on the old chalkboard," Henry added. "I'm sure she doesn't want the others to know about the furniture in the school."

Jessie grabbed her notebook off the kitchen counter and made some notes. "Martha is definitely a suspect," she said. "But then...she seemed really upset when she saw the message on the chalkboard in Room 214 today. I don't think she wrote that warning."

"Then who wrote it?" Benny asked.

Violet shrugged. "Maybe there's another suspect."

"What about Ansel?" Henry said. "He keeps showing up with his camera right after each strange thing that happens at the school."

"Also, remember when he said that he wanted the school to stay exactly the way it is?" Jessie asked.

"Maybe he's trying to stop the renovation," Violet said. "But why?"

They were all silent for a moment as they thought. But nobody had any answers.

Henry closed the laptop and folded his hands in his lap. He leaned back in his chair.

"I think it's time to search for more clues," he said. "We should begin first thing Saturday morning."

Benny nodded. "But there's just one thing," he said.

"What is it?" Jessie asked.

"Can we have some tapioca pudding first?" Benny asked.

\*\*\*

The Aldens were ready to leave the house two hours earlier than usual on Saturday morning. They'd asked Grandfather to take them to the Greenfield Public Library. The air was still crisp and cool when they got into the minivan.

"Hopefully we can get some answers today," Jessie said, as she tucked her notebook into her backpack.

Once they were in the library, Jessie pointed to

the second-floor stairway that led to the Periodicals department.

"Let's check out old newspaper articles," she said. "Maybe we can find out more about the Hawthorne School ghost."

The Aldens found a computer station that they could use to look up digital copies of every issue published by the Silver City and Greenfield newspapers. Henry typed HAWTHORNE SCHOOL into the search box, and a dozen articles appeared on the screen. Jessie read the first one aloud.

"'Hawthorne School Bake Sale Next Friday,'" she said. "That was March 19, 1948."

"Mmm, a bake sale sounds good," Benny said.

Henry smiled and ruffled Benny's hair. "It sure does," Henry agreed.

"Here's another story from the 1940s," Jessie said, pointing to a headline that read "Hawthorne School Modernizes First-Floor Classrooms." "That must have been when they covered up that old blackboard."

Henry read the short article. "Interesting. But nothing about the Hawthorne School ghost."

# Unusual Business

They read a few more articles, one headlined "Fund-Raiser for Hawthorne School PTA" and another about the winner of an essay contest. But there was nothing about a principal who had been fired, and nothing at all about a curse or a ghost.

Benny yawned.

"I'm starting to wonder how anyone got the idea that Hawthorne School was haunted," Violet said. "Nothing interesting ever happened there!"

"Oh, I don't know," said Jessie, pointing to a headline. "According to this story, a photography darkroom was added to one of the classrooms in 1952. That's kind of cool."

"But it doesn't explain the ghost," Henry reminded them. He scrolled down to look at more stories.

"This one is sort of sad," he said. "It's about a Hawthorne student named Hyacinth Weaver," Henry said.

"Hyacinth," Violet repeated. "Like the kind of flower?"

Henry nodded. "The article says her parents owned Weaver's Flower Shop in Silver City. In spring 1955, Hyacinth had to get her tonsils taken out and missed the last week of school." He pointed to a black-and-white photo. It showed a young girl standing outside her parents' flower shop.

"That's *all*?" Jessie said. "She missed the *last week of school*?"

"But that's the best week of all!" Benny said.

Everyone laughed at that.

"There's one more article here, from later that summer," Jessie said. The headline read, "Hawthorne School's Doors Close for Good!"

"It says that the school wouldn't be reopening in the fall," Henry said, after reading the article. "Hawthorne School didn't have enough students anymore, so it was combined with Greenfield School. And since Greenfield had a bigger and newer school building, students had to go there instead of returning to Hawthorne."

Jessie wrote the date the school closed in her notebook: *June 10, 1955.*

"Well, that's it," she said. "Let's go meet Grandfather."

Grandfather was on the first floor of the library,

standing next to the information center with a hardcover book tucked under his arm.

"Ready?" he asked.

The children nodded and walked with him to the minivan.

As they headed to Hawthorne School, Henry turned to his siblings.

"Do you think we've reached a dead end?" he asked them.

"It does seem strange that we didn't find any articles on the former principal," Violet said. "But I guess that means that story isn't true. And that there's no ghost."

"I thought we'd find something more interesting about the school," Jessie said.

"We only know about the bake sale," Benny added sadly. "And that was a long time ago."

When they reached the school, the Aldens climbed out of the minivan. They waved to Grandfather as he drove away.

"Let's check in with Bob," Henry suggested. "See where he needs us to help out today."

They looked up and down the hallways and in

each classroom, but they couldn't find Bob.

"There's Ansel," Benny said, pointing down the hallway. "Maybe he knows where Bob went."

They watched as Ansel turned a corner and then was out of sight.

Violet gasped.

"What is it?" Jessie asked.

"I—I just remembered something from the articles at the library," Violet said. "I think I know where Ansel is headed. And it might be a clue!"

"How?" Henry asked.

"Follow me!" Violet said. And with that, she took off running in the direction Ansel had gone.

# Behind the Curtain

Henry, Jessie, and Benny ran after Violet. They caught up with her outside Room 108.

"In here!" she said.

Everyone followed Violet into the room. It was empty.

"Nobody's here," Jessie said. She spun around a few times to make sure she wasn't missing anything.

"Did Ansel vanish?" Benny asked as he peeked under a desk.

"Of course not," Violet said. "I know where to find him." She walked over to a long curtain hanging in the corner of the room. It was made of dark, heavy velvet fabric, which she pulled back. Behind it was a tall, black pillar.

"What's that?" Benny asked, pointing at the pillar.

"It's a *door*," Violet said. "A special one."

The black pillar didn't look like a door at all. But Violet reached around it and found a small handle, which she pulled. The side of the pillar began to move, making a rolling noise.

"It *is* a door!" Jessie said with a gasp. "A curved, sliding door!"

The black door was a little bit like a revolving door in a store. They peered into what seemed to be a round closet.

"But what is it?" Henry asked.

"It's the door to the photography darkroom!" Violet exclaimed. "The one that was built in 1952! We read about it at the library this morning." Violet knew all about darkrooms. She had once taken a photography class and had used a door just like this one.

"So how do we get into the darkroom?" Jessie asked. This big, round black thing didn't look anything like a door. *No wonder nobody noticed it,* she thought.

"I'll show you," Violet replied. She stepped into the little round closet and motioned for the others to join her. "Now turn around and face the back," she said. As they did, she slid the curving door. The side of the closet that had been open to Room 108 now slid closed, and for a moment it was completely dark.

"Hang on," said Violet. She kept sliding the door until another room opened up—one on the other side. This room was lit by a glowing red light.

"I get it," Henry whispered. "The special round door lets you get to this red room without ever letting in the light from Room 108."

"Yes," Violet said. "Because the light would ruin the photographs."

"She's right!" said Ansel, his voice coming from the red-lit room. He was standing at a table and swishing a photograph around in a pan filled with liquid.

"Welcome to the darkroom," he said. "I've just printed a new photo. You can watch it develop."

The children went over to the table as Ansel picked up a pair of tongs. He used them to hold down photograph paper in a pan of processing solution. After a few moments in the solution, the blank paper changed to show a black-and-white image of Hawthorne School. The photograph was beautiful. Then Ansel dipped his tongs into the pan and pulled out the photograph. He moved it into another pan of liquid, then rinsed it in a third pan and clipped it to a line to dry.

Several other photographs hung alongside it. Each one was a different shot of the school. One was a close-up of an intricate wood carving that Violet recognized from the banister in the front hallway. Another showed the overgrown yard behind the school. The bare trees looked like skeletons. Ansel's photos were all in just black and white, and they looked dark and mysterious.

"I had always heard about the darkroom," Ansel said. "So I looked for it the first time I came here with my dad."

"The night that we met you," Violet said.

Ansel nodded. "The equipment is in pretty good shape," he continued. "I've been printing my own photos here since the renovation started."

Jessie noticed the darkroom was neat and tidy. Ansel had taken special care to keep everything orderly.

"I'd always used a digital camera," Ansel explained. He pointed to a few different types of cameras on a shelf. "But then I started to experiment with traditional photography. This darkroom gave me the perfect opportunity to develop my own pictures."

"When we first met, you said you wanted to keep Hawthorne School the way it is," Jessie said.

Ansel furrowed his brow for a moment and swished another photograph around in the liquid. "I did say that, didn't I?"

"That's right," Henry said. "So you don't want Hawthorne School to be renovated into an art center?"

"That's not what I meant," Ansel replied. "I'm excited about having an art center. But I love how old and spooky the school is, and I was worried that the renovation would change that. I shouldn't have worried though...It's still as spooky as ever around here!"

**Behind the Curtain**

The Aldens laughed along with him.

"And now," Ansel continued, "I have all of these photographs to show the school at its spookiest. I want to create a gallery to showcase them during the grand opening. It's important for people in Silver City to remember the history of old buildings like this one."

"That's a great idea," Henry said.

"Do you want to see some of the photos I've taken around the school?" Ansel asked.

The Aldens nodded enthusiastically. Ansel opened a drawer and pulled out a case. Inside was a binder full of black-and-white photos slid into clear plastic sleeves. The Aldens admired the photos. Ansel had captured the school's ghostly setting, but the images were also creative and beautiful.

"This one is very interesting," Violet said. She lifted the page to inspect the image.

"I like the way the locker doors are casting shadows in the hallway," Ansel replied.

In the photograph, all of the old locker doors were open. Violet noticed the lock dials were built into the doors. Their unique shape, combined with the lighting, made interesting shadows.

"Thanks for showing us your photos," Henry said. "And good luck getting everything done in time for the grand opening."

"Let us know if you need any help," Jessie added.

Ansel smiled. "I will."

Violet led everyone back through the small round closet and into Room 108. They sat down while Jessie took out her notebook.

"Now we know that Ansel isn't a suspect," Jessie said. She drew a line through Ansel's name in her notebook.

"And we know that a ghost didn't lock the door," Jessie said.

"Yes," Violet agreed. "When the volunteer was sweeping in here, she must not have known the darkroom door was there."

"Because it doesn't even look like a door!" Benny said.

"Right," said Violet. "She left the room for a few minutes. When she returned, Ansel must have locked the door!"

"And he left later that night," Jessie added. "So the door was unlocked the next morning."

"So it wasn't a ghost!" Benny exclaimed. "It was just Ansel."

The Alden children looked at one another.

"This explains what happened in Room 108," Violet said. "But who is behind the warning on the chalkboard in Room 214?"

# CHAPTER 8

# An Unexpected Discovery

"Benny," Henry said, sweeping up a pile of dust, "will you hand me the dustpan?"

The Aldens were in the old auditorium, where their job was to sweep the floor. It needed to be clean for a fresh coat of paint. The art committee had asked local artists to design an emblem that would be painted on the floor. Bob had shown them a drawing of the design, which featured a beautiful *H*, *A*, and *C* for Hawthorne Art Center.

Cleaning the auditorium was one of the Aldens' final volunteer tasks. They were impressed by the way the school was shaping up. Cobwebs had been brushed out of corners and crooks. Even tiny holes had been patched. And the walls were now painted a pristine white. Doorknobs were dusted and polished. Henry had even helped fix the flagpole. Now the flag waved and rippled in the wind, greeting everyone each day. Of course, some major work still needed to be done. The lockers had to be removed, and not all of the electrical work was finished. Even so, the school looked brighter and cleaner than ever.

But above and beyond the excitement around the renovations, the Aldens were looking forward to the grand opening party...and then participating in all of the programs the new art center offered!

Benny crouched down to hold the dustpan while Henry swept a heap of dirt into it.

"For being so old, the auditorium is in great shape," Henry said. He looked around and was impressed.

"Ansel made a good point," Violet said from the stage. "Trying to keep the school's history alive in the renovation was a great idea. This building is so cool. It didn't need to be torn down!"

Behind Violet, Jessie bent down to wipe a smudge off the stage floor. She shook her head as she noticed muddy footprints leading offstage. Jessie wiped up the dirty tracks one by one.

The Alden children were so focused on their tasks that they didn't notice someone else was in the auditorium. But then they heard a voice.

"I can assure you," the woman said, "I am the first antique dealer to visit this school."

Jessie looked around and didn't see anyone. But she recognized the voice right away...It was Martha! Violet and Benny also looked around. Henry just shrugged.

"I bet the sound acoustics are really good in here," he explained. "After all, it is an auditorium, and the audience needs to be able to hear actors and musicians well."

"Where is she?" Benny asked.

"She's probably off in the wings somewhere," Jessie replied. "It sounds like she's talking on her cell phone."

Everyone went back to sweeping and wiping the floor. But they still heard Martha's conversation.

"I even scouted out the best pieces before the renovation started," Martha continued.

There was a long pause before she spoke again.

"No," she said firmly. "I've changed my mind about trying any more tricks to snap up the best pieces."

Another pause. Martha was listening to the person on the other end of the line.

"There's weird energy here," she finally said with a shaky voice. "I'll do my best to get good pieces, but from now on, I'm doing business fairly."

Martha said good-bye to her customer and ended the call. When she pulled back the curtain to the stage, she was startled to see the Aldens working.

"I didn't realize anyone was here!" she said.

"We're just finishing," Henry replied.

"Yes," Martha said as she looked around. "You all have done a really nice job here. The new art center will be ready in no time!"

Jessie raised her eyebrows as a thought occurred to her.

"We heard you talking," she started. She pointed to the cell phone in Martha's hand. "And you said that you checked out the place before you started working here. When was that?"

# An Unexpected Discovery

Martha hesitated for a moment, as if not sure whether to tell the children the truth. Finally, she spoke. "It was the same night you were here. The night you met Bob," she admitted. "I found a flyer about the renovation project and came to the school to have a look."

Martha rummaged through her bag and pulled out a yellow piece of paper. She handed it to Henry. It was the same flyer Grandfather had found that led the Aldens to the Hawthorne School renovation.

"So," Henry said. He thought back to the first time they met Bob. "You knew who we were before we officially met on the first day of work. And you knew Watch too!"

Martha nodded and smiled.

"I was upstairs while you were walking through the classrooms," she said. "After you left for the playground, I slipped out the front door."

It all made sense now. Watch had been so jumpy that night because he sensed Martha's presence. And it also explained why the Aldens had the eerie feeling that someone was watching them. Someone was...Martha!

"Why did you keep it a secret?" Benny asked.

"I didn't want any other dealers to find out about all of the great antiques here," Martha replied.

Violet perked up as Martha explained her story. She remembered the rumor about furniture being moved in the school. Several volunteers thought the Hawthorne School ghost was responsible for desks and chairs that had been found in odd places. Now Violet thought that Martha could have done it.

"Did you move any of the furniture?" Violet asked.

"I did move some," Martha admitted. "I was hoping to save some of the best pieces, so I could be the first to bid on them at the auction. If someone else found them, they would be eager to bid before me."

The Aldens followed Martha to the edge of the stage. They all sat down and swung their legs over the ledge. Martha seemed less mysterious now. Over the past few weeks, she had simply been trying to find antique furniture. Jessie looked at a page in her notebook. Everything that Martha said seemed to add up. But she still had one last question.

# An Unexpected Discovery

"Martha, did you write the spooky message on the chalkboard in Room 214?" Jessie asked her.

Martha's eyes grew wide. "No!" she said. "I didn't write that message. I wish I knew who did though. It gives me the creeps." She crossed her arms and shivered.

The Aldens looked at one another. Martha had definitely acted strangely in the past. But now they knew her reasons. And something about the frightened look on her face made Jessie think that Martha was telling the truth when she said she hadn't written the spooky message. Jessie crossed her name off the list of suspects.

"We believe you," Jessie told Martha.

Henry and Jessie stood up and grabbed the brooms they had propped up against the wall. To their surprise, Martha also reached for a broom.

"It's time I started helping," she said, swishing the broom across the floor. Once she had a neat pile of dirt, Benny crouched down with his dustpan. In no time, they were nearly done cleaning the auditorium's floor.

"Thanks for your help," Violet told Martha.

Martha then grabbed a cloth and helped Jessie wipe scuffs and scrapes off the floor. They were busily cleaning when the auditorium door opened. They saw Mrs. Koslowski walking down the aisle. She was eyeing their progress, but she seemed like she had other things on her mind.

"Hi, Mrs. K," Henry said. "Can we help you with anything?"

"Hello," she replied. She waved quickly to the children. "No, I don't need any help."

Martha handed Jessie her dust cloth.

"I think we're done here," Martha said, looking at the spotless floor. "I'll take a walk with Hyacinth."

"Hyacinth?" Jessie asked. "Mrs. K's first name is...Hyacinth?"

"Hyacinth," Benny repeated. "Like the flower!"

"Lovely, isn't it?" Martha replied, smiling. "Her family owned Silver City's oldest florist. Have you seen Weaver's Flower Shop on Main Street? And Benny's right. She was named after her father's favorite flower."

Martha stepped off the stage and made her way to Mrs. Koslowski. The two of them walked out of the auditorium.

Jessie spun around to face her brothers and sister.

"Did you hear that?" she asked.

"Mrs. K is the girl from that newspaper article!" Henry exclaimed.

"The one who had her tonsils out and missed the last week of school!" Violet said.

"Wait a second..." Jessie flipped through her notebook, running her finger down each page as she scanned her notes. "That last week of school that she missed? It was also *the last week that Hawthorne School was ever open!*"

"That's true," Violet said. "All of the students had to go to Greenfield School that fall. I bet she missed her chance to say good-bye to her old classrooms. That might be why she's been wandering through the halls."

"Benny's right," Henry said. "The last week of school is always the best."

Jessie nodded. She remembered last June, when she and her friends had cleaned out their lockers. On the last day of school, they'd gathered their belongings to take home. That way, the school was clean and empty, ready for the next year.

"She didn't get to take her things home," Henry said. "They've been locked up here all these years."

Suddenly, Jessie looked up from her notebook. Her eyes lit up, as if she'd figured something out.

"Follow me," she said.

They followed Jessie back into the main school building. She raced up the stairs to the second floor. When she finally reached Room 214, she abruptly stopped.

As they entered the room, they saw the mysterious message still written on the chalkboard.

*Stay away! Whoever dares unlock my secret will be sorry...*

"Do you see?" Jessie asked. She excitedly pointed to the chalkboard.

"Yes!" Henry said. "Mrs. K must be trying to find her old locker. Her things have been locked away for sixty years!"

"So," Violet said. "Now we know."

Benny nodded. "Mrs. K wrote the mystery message!"

## CHAPTER

9

# Unlocking the Past

"It all makes sense!" Jessie exclaimed.

The Aldens continued to stare at the message Mrs. Koslowski had written on the chalkboard. The curvy, elegant handwritten letters spelled out the spooky words in the warning to stay away.

"Mrs. K must have wanted to find her things before someone else did," Violet said. "She was probably worried they would go into the trash. Then they would be gone forever."

Everyone agreed with Violet. Mrs. K wasn't absentminded; she was just very focused on finding the things she had left in her locker all those years ago.

"She did a great job copying the writing we

found on the chalkboard in Room 108," Henry said. He remembered that Mrs. K said the writing resembled her mother's penmanship. She must have used it as a guide when writing the note.

"We could just ask Mrs. K about it," Jessie suggested.

"We could help her find her things," Benny said.

Henry walked over to the old wooden table sitting in the middle of the room. He pulled out a chair and sat down.

"But every time we've seen her wandering the halls and ask her if she's looking for something, she's denied it," Henry said.

Jessie sat down at the table next to him.

"Maybe she doesn't want to bother anyone," Jessie said.

Violet and Benny also sat down at the table.

"If she doesn't find her things fast," Violet said, "it might be too late."

Henry nodded. "You're right," he said.

"And the renovation is in the final stage," Jessie added. "All the lockers will be torn out to allow room for the new gallery hall. All of the lockers will be thrown out...and everything in them!"

"We have to help Mrs. K," Violet said. "But how?"

"That's easy," Benny replied. "All we have to do is find the locked locker!"

They took turns high-fiving Benny for his clever idea. If they found the locker that had not been opened since the last day of school in 1955, they would surely find Mrs. Koslowski's hidden belongings.

"OK," Henry said. "Here's the plan."

He drew an outline of the school on a piece of loose-leaf paper.

"We'll have to divide into teams to tackle all of the lockers," he continued. "Jessie and Violet will take the first floor. Benny and I will take the lockers on the second floor. We'll meet here in an hour."

Henry pointed to a spot on the map directly in front of Room 108.

"Let's go," Jessie said, standing. "Let's find Mrs. K's long-lost things!"

Jessie and Violet headed downstairs to the lockers on the first floor. The red lockers looked old and dingy.

"Let's start with the top ones," Jessie suggested. The lockers were arranged in two rows, one on top of the other.

The sisters pulled the handle of each locker door. Every one opened easily.

"Now for the bottom row," Violet said.

After opening and closing each locker, the Alden sisters determined that Mrs. Koslowski's locker was not on the first floor.

Upstairs, Henry and Benny were not having much luck either. Each locker pulled open right away.

"It's getting late," Henry said. "We should head to Room 108."

Benny looked down the hallway at the unopened lockers. The second floor held several more rows than the first floor. Henry and Benny had not yet finished checking them.

"What if we never find Mrs. K's locker?" Benny asked as they walked down the flight of stairs to the first floor.

"We'll just have to keep trying," Henry replied.

As they turned the corner, they saw Jessie and

Violet standing in front of Room 108. They were talking to Ansel.

"Look who we ran into," Jessie said.

"Ansel was just leaving the darkroom for the day," Violet added.

# Hidden in the Haunted School

Henry asked Ansel about his project. Everyone wanted to know if he had found more interesting scenes to photograph.

"I've been playing more with the lighting and shadows from the open lockers," Ansel replied.

"Open lockers?" Jessie asked. "Did *all* of the lockers open?"

"As a matter of fact," Ansel replied, "one of them was locked."

"Mrs. K's locker!" Benny cheered.

The Alden children excitedly told Ansel about the old newspaper story and how they thought the locked locker was Mrs. Koslowski's.

"Where is the locker?" Henry asked.

Ansel explained that there was a short hallway on the second floor, off to the side of the main hall. It could be easily missed, if someone didn't know about it. The locked locker was in this nook.

"We must have missed it," Henry said. "We'll go check it out right now."

"And I'll find Mrs. K and bring her upstairs," Ansel said. "We'll all meet in front of the locker."

"Mrs. K will be so surprised!" Violet said.

# Unlocking the Past

Ansel went around the corner while the Aldens went up to the second floor, following Ansel's directions to the locker. Sure enough, there was a small hallway off the main hall. A few lockers lined the walls. Jessie took a deep breath and tried to open the very last one. It was locked!

"We found it!" Benny cried with delight.

"Now we wait," Jessie said.

A few minutes passed, but there was no sign of Ansel and Mrs. K. It was now late in the afternoon. They could see the sun dipping below the horizon out the window, and the light in the hallway was growing dim and shadowy. Jessie flipped on the light switch, but only a few bulbs glowed in the murky darkness. The other bulbs were cracked and broken. Henry had brought a battery-powered lantern to help look inside the lockers, and he held it up to give them some light, but it only helped a little bit. All around them in the gloomy hallway they could recognize the dark shapes and shadows from Ansel's photographs.

Violet shivered. "I can see why Ansel likes to photograph here," she said. "It sure is spooky."

Jessie nodded and hugged her arms to her chest.

"What if we're wrong about Mrs. K playing pranks?" Violet asked.

"What if there really is a ghost?" Benny continued.

Henry was about to tell Benny there was no such thing as a ghost at Hawthorne School. But then the Aldens heard the sound of a shut door rattling.

"What was that?" Violet asked.

A few moments passed. The door rattled again.

Jessie pointed to a dark doorway at the end of the hall. "It's coming from there," she said, her voice shaking a little.

The four of them were all thinking the same thing.

*What if the legend of the Hawthorne School ghost was true after all?*

# A Grand Opening

Just then, Benny stepped away from the lockers and stood in the center of the hallway. He crossed his arms.

"We can't be scared. We have to find Mrs. K," he said. "She's looking for something important."

"Benny's right," Henry said. "We have to see what's going on."

He led the way down the hallway, taking a second to peek into the open door of each classroom. All the rooms were empty. Finally, they reached the dark end of the hall...and the closed door.

Henry hesitated in front of the door.

"We have to open it!" Benny said. He stepped forward and placed his hand on the doorknob.

"For being so small, you sure are brave!" Violet told him.

Benny turned the knob and pulled it open, squeezing his eyes closed as he did. If there was a ghost, he didn't want to see it!

"Thank goodness!" cried Mrs. K, who stood with Ansel and Bob behind the door. "We came up the back stairs, but this door wouldn't open!"

Jessie let out a sigh of relief as the adults came into the hallway.

"I understand you have something to show me?" Mrs. K asked.

"Yes!" Benny exclaimed. "Come on!"

"Wait a moment," said Mrs. K. "Let me sit down for a moment. I need to tell you all something."

Bob found a chair from one of the classrooms and brought it over to Mrs. K. She gently sat down. She removed her glasses and blinked a few times. Then she pulled a tissue out of her pocket and nervously began cleaning the lenses of her glasses.

"I'm terribly sorry," she started. "I had no idea my little message would get this out of hand. Everybody was talking about the Hawthorne ghost, and I thought the warning might buy me a little time to find my things."

She put her glasses back on. Mrs. K appeared to be more bashful than usual. She took a deep breath and then fiddled with her glasses again.

"We know you were searching for your old locker," Henry said. "You must have left something in there."

"You had to leave school to have your tonsils taken out," Jessie continued.

"But then the next year, you went to Greenfield School," Violet said.

"So you never got your things from your locker!" Benny finished.

"Yes...yes, it's all true," Mrs. K said.

The Alden children watched as Mrs. Koslowski relaxed. Bob brought her a bottle of water. She slowly sipped it.

"A week before I went into the hospital, my grandmother gave me a bracelet—a token of good luck," Mrs. K finally said. "It was gold with tiny amethyst crystals. My birthstone...and also my grandmother's birthstone. I was so proud of it I

brought it to school to show my friends! But then...
I forgot it."

"Hyacinth explained that the bracelet is very
precious to her," Bob said. "Not because of its cost,
but because it came from her grandmother!"

Mrs. Koslowski nodded. She touched her wrist,
as if she was stroking an imaginary piece of jewelry.

"I'm sure the volunteers will understand," Jessie
said. "Maybe you could tell them your story."

"And then they'll know there is no such thing as
the Hawthorne ghost!" Benny added.

Mrs. K brightened. "Bob," she said. "Do you
think you could gather the volunteers? I'd like to
apologize to them!"

Everyone smiled. Bob said he would call a
volunteer meeting for the following day. Mrs. K
would have her chance to tell them how sorry she
was for scaring them during the renovations.

Henry turned to Mrs. K. "Now," he said. "Let's
get your things."

Mrs. K jumped to her feet. She followed Henry as
he led the way down the hallway. She had a spring
in her step.

# A Grand Opening

"This is it," Jessie said, pointing to the shut locker. She spun the dial a few times. Then she asked Mrs. Koslowski for the combination.

"I'm not sure I remember it," Mrs. K replied. "I didn't even remember my locker was here."

She called out a few numbers as Jessie turned the dial. Each combination turned out to be wrong. The locker was still shut tight.

"Did you use a special date as the combination?" Henry asked. "For my school locker, I use the day, month, and last two digits of the year we met Grandfather. That way, I always remember it."

"Yes, that's right," Mrs. Koslowski replied. "My grandmother's birthday. Try this, Jessie..."

She recited three more sets of numbers. This time, the dial clicked, and the locker opened. Mrs. Koslowski reached inside and pulled out a small box. Opening it, she revealed a beautiful, sparkling gold bracelet with soft purple gemstones. Violet helped Mrs. K clasp it around her wrist.

"What else is in there?" Benny asked.

"Let's see," she replied. She reached into the locker again and pulled out some old school

supplies and a pencil case. Everyone chose an item to examine.

"It's like we opened a time capsule!" Jessie exclaimed.

She was holding one of Mrs. K's old school folders. On the front, several animated characters were cheerfully giving the thumbs-up sign.

"Look at these," Henry said as he turned over a

few coins in his hand. Although old, the coins were shiny and bright from being tucked away in the dark locker.

Mrs. K turned to Benny. "Oh dear," she said, seeing the small plastic horse he was holding. "That's a toy from my favorite TV show. I'd forgotten all about these things. Finding them now is like taking a trip down memory lane!"

Under a few schoolbooks, they discovered an old newspaper that had been stashed away in the locker. The Alden children took turns reading the current events from 1955.

Everyone was excited that Mrs. K had finally found her belongings. Bob even suggested featuring them in the new display case.

"What a wonderful idea," Mrs. K replied.

Violet nodded enthusiastically. "This way," she said, "everyone who visits the art center will know what school was like in the fifties."

The Alden children knew that Grandfather would arrive soon to pick them up. As they said good night to Bob, Ansel, and Mrs. K, she turned to them one last time.

"Thank you!" she called. And then she descended the back staircase and was out of sight.

***

Grandfather and the Alden children stood on the stone steps of the new Hawthorne Art Center. They looked up at the old building with astonishment. It was hardly the spooky school they had found months earlier while running their weekend errands. In fact, although the sun was setting, the area was lit up. Several streetlamps had been added to the parking lot, and small lanterns lined the path to the front door. Inside the building, all of the broken lights had been fixed. The old school glowed brightly. The renovations were complete.

Grandfather opened the newly painted red door and ushered the children inside. A large banner in the entrance hall read, GRAND OPENING PARTY!

Henry looked around. "Wow!" he said. "Everything looks great. It's like a brand-new building."

Violet gazed up at the grand trophy case, now without the cobwebs. The old trophies had been polished and looked beautiful.

"Yes," she said. "And it still has all of the details

that made Hawthorne School so special."

Bob spotted the Aldens and welcomed them to the party. As Grandfather chatted with him, the Alden children continued to walk through the art center. They marveled at how much it had changed.

They came to Room 108. Instantly, they recognized the photographs hanging on the walls inside the room. They were the black-and-white pictures Ansel had taken before the renovations were finished. They turned out to be spooky and artistic—just as he had hoped. Violet found a sign-up sheet for photography lessons. She put her name on the list. She couldn't wait to start taking her own photographs.

Next door, the antique chalkboard was now behind a plastic case. The old-fashioned lessons and curvy handwriting were preserved for everyone to see.

They walked upstairs to find that the hall was now a gallery space. There was room for drawings and sculptures to be displayed.

"It's a good thing Mrs. K found her things when she did," Jessie noted. "She almost lost them forever."

As the others nodded, they heard someone walk up behind them.

"And I owe it all to you," Mrs. K said.

The children turned to see Mrs. Koslowski. They noticed right away that she was wearing her purple and gold bracelet. After a few minutes of catching up, Henry asked if she ever spoke to the other volunteers. He wondered if she'd had the chance to tell them about the strange message she wrote on the chalkboard.

"Oh yes," she said. "Bob called a meeting for the next day. I put the Hawthorne ghost rumor to rest once and for all!"

Everyone was thrilled with the good news. They said good-bye to Mrs. K and headed back downstairs to look for Grandfather. He was still standing with Bob. As they joined them, Ansel and Martha also approached.

"Your photographs are wonderful," Violet told him. "We saw them hanging in Room 108."

"Thanks!" Ansel replied. "You should see the darkroom. It's all fixed up and ready for photography students to use."

Violet smiled, knowing she would soon have the chance to test it out herself.

Jessie turned to Martha. "How is your antique business?" she asked.

Martha couldn't wait to tell them all about it. When the furniture finally went to auction, she was the first bidder. All of the furniture sold quickly.

"Except," she said, "for a very special piece. I saved this for myself..."

Martha pulled out her cell phone and showed them a photo of the old clock.

"It's now fixed and works perfectly!" she said.

Bob turned his attention to the children. "What do you think of the new art center?" he asked.

"It's perfect," Jessie replied.

"There's just one thing missing," Benny said.

Bob looked puzzled. "What's that?" he asked.

"The snack tent!" Benny replied.

Everyone laughed.

# THE BOXCAR CHILDREN®

GREAT ADVENTURE

## A Brand-New 5-Book Miniseries

**Henry, Jessie, Violet, and Benny Alden are on a secret mission that takes them around the world!**

When Violet finds a turtle statue that nobody's seen before in an old trunk at home, the children are on the case! The clue turns out to be an invitation to the Reddimus Society, a secret guild dedicated to returning lost treasures to where they belong.

Now the Aldens must take the statue and six mysterious boxes across the country to deliver them safely—and keep them out of the hands of the Reddimus Society's enemies. It's just the beginning of the Boxcar Children's most amazing adventure yet!

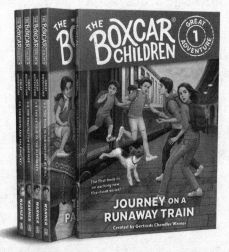

**#1: Journey on a Runaway Train**
HC 978-0-8075-0695-0 · PB 978-0-8075-0696-7

**#2: The Clue in the Papyrus Scroll**
HC 978-0-8075-0698-1 · PB 978-0-8075-0699-8

**#3: The Detour of the Elephants**
HC 978-0-8075-0684-4 · PB 978-0-8075-0685-1

**#4: The Shackleton Sabotage**
HC 978-0-8075-0687-5 · PB 978-0-8075-0688-2

**#5: The Khipu and the Final Key**
HC 978-0-8075-0681-3 · PB 978-0-8075-0682-0

**GERTRUDE CHANDLER WARNER** discovered when she was teaching that many readers who like an exciting story could find no books that were both easy and fun to read. She decided to try to meet this need, and her first book, *The Boxcar Children*, quickly proved she had succeeded.

Miss Warner drew on her own experiences to write the mystery. As a child she spent hours watching trains go by on the tracks opposite her family home. She often dreamed about what it would be like to set up housekeeping in a caboose or freight car—the situation the Alden children find themselves in.

While the mystery element is central to each of Miss Warner's books, she never thought of them as strictly juvenile mysteries. She liked to stress the Aldens' independence and resourcefulness and their solid New England devotion to using up and making do. The Aldens go about most of their adventures with as little adult supervision as possible— something else that delights young readers.

Miss Warner lived in Putnam, Connecticut, until her death in 1979. During her lifetime, she received hundreds of letters from girls and boys telling her how much they liked her books.

# THE BOXCAR CHILDREN®

**The Boxcar Children investigate shadowy figures, nighttime disappearances, and haunted hallways in three eerie adventures!**

### THE MYSTERY OF THE STOLEN SWORD

The Aldens visit an apple orchard that's rumored to be haunted. Soon they learn that some of the owner's antiques have gone missing. Is the thief someone at the orchard, or is it a ghost coming to reclaim what is his?

### THE VAMPIRE MYSTERY

Rumors of a vampire in the town's graveyard are keeping people away from Greenfield. Could the strange events have something to do with the local author who is best known for his vampire stories?

### HIDDEN IN THE HAUNTED SCHOOL

The Boxcar Children volunteer to help clean up an abandoned school. But strange events keep scaring off the other volunteers. Why is someone—or something—trying to keep people away?

## ALBERT WHITMAN & COMPANY

*Publishing award-winning children's books since 1919*

www.albertwhitman.com • www.boxcarchildren.com

Cover art by Anthony VanArsdale
Printed in the United States of America

978-0-8075-2848-8 • $9.99

5 0 9 9 9

9 780807 528488

**It's more than just a mystery.**